The Day
The Cisco Kid
Shot John Wayne

Bilingual Press/Editorial Bilingüe

General Editor
Gary D. Keller

Managing Editor
Karen S. Van Hooft

Senior Editor
Mary M. Keller

Assistant Editor
Linda St. George Thurston

Editorial Board
Juan Goytisolo
Francisco Jiménez
Eduardo Rivera
Severo Sarduy
Mario Vargas Llosa

Address
Bilingual Review/Press
Hispanic Research Center
Arizona State University
Tempe, Arizona 85287
(602) 965-3867

The Day
The Cisco Kid
Shot John Wayne

Nash Candelaria

Bilingual Press/Editorial Bilingüe
TEMPE, ARIZONA

ISBN: 0-916950-81-6

Library of Congress Catalog Card Number: 88-70125

PRINTED IN THE UNITED STATES OF AMERICA

Cover design by Christopher J. Bidlack

Back cover photo by Andrea Cypress

Acknowledgments

This volume is supported by a grant from the National Endowment for
the Arts in Washington, D.C., a federal agency.

The editors wish to thank the following publications for permission to
reprint stories by Nash Candelaria that appear in this volume:

Puerto del Sol, for "Tío Ignacio's Stigmata," in Volume 16 (Spring 1981),
53-63.

The Americas Review (Revista Chicano-Riqueña), for "The Day the Cisco
Kid Shot John Wayne," in Volume XI, No. 2 (Summer 1983), 52-64; and
"Affirmative Action," in Volume XIV, Nos. 3-4 (Fall-Winter 1986),
11-18.

Rudolfo A. Anaya, for the editors of Cuentos Chicanos, A Short Story
Anthology, eds. Rudolfo A. Anaya and Antonio Márquez, for "El
Patrón" (Albuquerque, NM: University of New Mexico Press, 1984),
41-47.

Other stories by Nash Candelaria included in this volume first appeared in
the following publications:

"Carnitas y huesitos," in De Colores, Volume 5, Nos. 3 & 4, 1981, 34-42.
"Be-Bop Rock," in Riversedge, Volume IV, No. 2 (May 1982), 71-80.

This volume includes satirical fiction which is not to be taken as an
assertion of actual fact about any individual named herein.

Contents

Novels by Nash Candelaria

The Rafa trilogy:

Memories of the Alhambra
Not by the Sword
Inheritance of Strangers

The Day the Cisco Kid Shot John Wayne

Just before I started the first grade we moved from Los Rafas into town. It created a family uproar that left hard feelings for a long time.

"You think you're too good for us," Uncle Luis shouted at Papa in Spanish, "just because you finished high school and have a job in town! My God! We grew up in the country. Our parents and grandparents grew up in the country. If New Mexico country was good enough for them—"

Papa stood with his cup and saucer held tightly in his hands, his knuckles bleached by the vicious grip as if all the blood had been squeezed up to his bright red face. But even when angry, he was polite to his older brother.

"I'll be much closer to work, and Josie can have the car to shop once in awhile. We'll still come out on weekends. It's only five miles."

Uncle Luis looked around in disbelief. My aunt tried not to look at either him or Papa, while Grandma sat on her rocking chair smoking a handrolled cigarette. She was blind and couldn't see the anger on the men's faces, but she wasn't deaf. Her chair started to rock faster, and I knew that in a moment she was going to scream at them both.

"It's much closer to work," Papa repeated.

Before Uncle Luis could shout again, Grandma blew out a puff of cigarette smoke in exasperation. "He's a grown man, Luis. With a wife and children. He can live anywhere he wants."

"But what about the—"

He was going to say orchard next to Grandma's house. It belonged to Papa and everyone expected him to build a house there someday. Grandma cut Uncle short, "Enough!"

As we bumped along the dirt of Rafas Road toward home in

the slightly used Ford we were all so proud of, Papa and Mama talked some more. It wasn't just being nearer to work, Papa said, but he couldn't tell the family because they wouldn't understand. It was time for Junior, that was me, to use English as his main language. He would get much better schooling in town than in the little country school where all the grades were in just two rooms.

"Times have changed," Papa said. "He'll have to live in the English-speaking world."

It surprised me. I was, it turned out, the real reason we were moving into town, and I felt a little unworthy. I also felt apprehensive about a new house, a new neighborhood, and my first year in school. Nevertheless, the third week in August we moved into the small house on Fruit Avenue not far from Immaculate Heart Parochial School.

I barely had time to acquaint myself with the neighborhood before school began. It was just as well. It was not like the country. Sidewalks were new to me, and I vowed to ask Santa Claus for roller skates at Christmas like those that city kids had. All of the streets were paved, not just the main highway like in the country. At night street lights blazed into life so you could see what was happening outside. It wasn't much. And the lights bothered me. I missed the secret warm darkness with its silence punctuated only by the night sounds of owls and crickets and frogs and distant dogs barking. Somehow the country dark had always been a friend, like a warm bed and being tucked in and being hugged and kissed good night.

There were no neighbors my age. The most interesting parts of the neighborhood were the vacant house next door and the vacant lot across the street. But then the rush to school left me no time to think or worry about neighbors.

I suppose I was a little smug, a little superior marching off that first day. My little sister and brother stood beside Aunt Tillie and watched anxiously through the front window, blocking their wide-eyed views with their steaming hot breaths. I shook off Mama's hand and shifted my new metal lunchbox to that side so she wouldn't try again.

Mama wanted to walk me into the classroom, but I wouldn't let her, even though I was frightened. On the steps in front of the old brick school building a melee of high voices said goodbye to mothers, interrupted by the occasional tearful face or clinging hand that refused to let go. At the corner of the entrance, leaning jauntily against the bricks, leered a brown-faced tough whose half-closed eyes singled me out. Even his wet, combed hair, scrubbed face, and neatly patched clothes did not disguise his true nature.

He stuck out a foot to trip me as I walked past. Like with my boy cousins in the country, I stepped on it good and hard without giving him even so much as a glance.

Sister Mary Margaret welcomed us to class. "You are here," she said, "as good Catholic children to learn your lessons well so you can better worship and glorify God." Ominous words in Anglo that I understood too well. I knew that cleanliness was next to godliness, but I never knew that learning your school lessons was—until then.

The students stirred restlessly, and during the turmoil I took a quick look around. It reminded me of a chocolate sundae. All the pale-faced Anglos were the vanilla ice cream, while we brown Hispanos were the sauce. The nun, with her starched white headdress under her cowl could have been the whipped cream except that I figured she was too sour for that.

I had never been among so many Anglo children before; they outnumbered us two to one. In the country church on Sundays it was rare to see an Anglo. The only time I saw many of these foreigners—except for a few friends of my father's—was when my parents took me into town shopping.

"One thing more," Sister Mary Margaret said. She stiffened, and her face turned to granite. It was the look that I later learned meant the ruler for some sinner's outstretched hands. Her hard eyes focused directly on me. "The language of this classroom is English. This is America. We will only speak English in class and on the school grounds." The warning hung ominously in the silent, crackling air. She didn't need to say what we brown-faces knew: If I hear Spanish, you're in trouble.

As we burst from the confines of the room for our first recess, I searched for that tough whose foot I had stomped on the way in. But surprise! He was not in our class. This puzzled me because I had thought there was only one first grade.

I found him out on the school ground though. Or rather, he found me. When he saw me, he swaggered across the playground tailed by a ragtag bunch of boys like odds and ends of torn cloth tied to a kite. One of the boys from my class whispered to me in English with an accent that sounded normal—only Anglos really had accents. "Oh, oh! Chango, the third grader. Don't let his size fool you. He can beat up guys twice as big." With which my classmate suddenly remembered something he had to do across the way by the water fountain.

"¡Ojos largos!" Chango shouted at me. I looked up in surprise. Not so much for the meaning of the words, which was "big eyes," but for his audacity is not only speaking Spanish against the nun's orders, but in shouting it in complete disregard of our jailers in black robes.

"Yes?" I said in English like an obedient student. I was afraid he would see my pounding heart bumping the cloth of my shirt.

Chango and his friends formed a semicircle in front of me. He placed his hands on his hips and thrust his challenging face at me, his words in the forbidden language. "Let's see you do that again."

"What?" I said in English, even though I knew what.

"And talk in Spanish," he hissed at me. "None of your highfalutin Anglo."

Warily I looked around to see if any of the nuns were nearby. "¿Qué?" I repeated when I saw that the coast was clear.

"You stepped on my foot, big eyes. And your big eyes are going to get it for that."

I shook my head urgently. "Not me," I said in all innocence. "It must have been somebody else."

But he knew better. In answer, he thrust a foot out and flicked his head at it in invitation. I stood my ground as if I didn't understand, and one of his orderlies laughed and hissed, "¡Gallina!"

The accusation angered me. I didn't like being called chicken, but a glance at the five of them waiting for me to do something did wonders for my self-restraint.

Then Chango swaggered forward, his arms out low like a wrestler's. He figured I was going to be easy, but I hadn't grown up with older cousins for nothing. When he feinted an arm at me, I stood my ground. At the next feint, I grabbed him with both hands, one on his wrist, the other at his elbow, and tripped him over my leg that snapped out like a jackknife. He landed flat on his behind, his face changing from surprise to anger and then to caution, all in an instant.

His cronies looked down at him for the order to jump me, but he ignored them. He bounced up immediately to show that it hadn't hurt or perhaps had been an accident and snarled, "Do that again."

I did. This time his look of surprise shaded into one of respect. His subordinates looked at each other in wonder and bewilderment. "He's only a first grader," one of them said. "Just think how tough he's going to be when he's older."

Meanwhile I was praying that Chango wouldn't ask me to do it a third time. I had a premonition that I had used up all of my luck. Somebody heard my prayer, because Chango looked up from the dirt and extended a hand. Was it an offer of friendship, or did he just want me to pull him to his feet?

To show that I was a good sport, I reached down. Instead of a shake or a tug up, he pulled me down so I sprawled alongside him. Everybody laughed.

"That's showing him, Chango," somebody said.

Then Chango grinned, and I could see why the nickname. With his brown face, small size, and simian smile there could be no other. "You wanna join our gang?" he asked. "I think you'll do." What if I say no? I thought. But the bell saved me because they started to amble back to class. "Meet us on the steps after school," Chango shouted. I nodded, brushing the dust from my cords as I hurried off.

That was how I became one of Los Indios, which was what we called ourselves. It was all pretty innocent, not at all what people think of when they see brown faces, hear Spanish words, and are told about "gangs." It was a club really, like any kid club. It made us more than nonentities. It was a recognition like the medal for bravery given to the cowardly lion in *The Wizard of Oz*.

What we mostly did was walk home together through enemy territory. Since we were Los Indios, it was the cowboys and the settlers we had to watch out for. The Anglo ones. Vaqueros y paisanos were OK. Also, it was a relief to slip into Spanish again

after guarding my tongue all day so it wouldn't incite Sister Mary
Margaret. It got so I even began to dream in English, and that
made me feel very uncomfortable as if I was betraying something very deep and ancient and basic.

Some of the times, too, there were fights. As I said before, we
were outnumbered two to one, and the sound of words in another language sometimes outraged other students, although
they didn't seem to think about that when we all prayed in Latin.
In our parish it was a twist on the old cliché: The students that
pray together fight together—against each other.

But there was more to Los Indios than that. Most important
there were the movies. I forget the name of the theatre. I think it
was the Río. But no matter. We called it the Rat House. When it
was very quiet during the scary part of the movie, just before the
villain was going to pounce on the heroine, you could hear the
scamper of little feet across the floor. We sat with our smelly
tennis shoes up on the torn seats—we couldn't have done any
more harm to those uncomfortable lumps. And one day someone swore he saw a large, gray furry something slither through
the cold, stale popcorn in the machine in the lobby. None of us
would ever have bought popcorn after that, even if we'd had the
money.

For a dime, though, you still couldn't beat the Rat House.
Saturday matinees were their specialty, although at night during
the week they showed Spanish language movies that parents and
aunts and uncles went to see. Saturdays, though, were for American westerns, monster movies, and serials.

Since I was one of the few who ever had money, I was initiat-
ed into a special assignment that first Saturday. I was the front
man, paying hard cash for a ticket that allowed me to hurry past
the candy counter—no point in being tempted by what you
couldn't get. I slipped down the left aisle near the screen where,
behind a half drawn curtain, was a door on which was painted
"Exit." No one could see the sign because the light bulb was
burned out, and they never replaced it in all the years we went
there. I guess they figured if the lights were too strong, the
patrons would see what a terrible wreck the theatre was and not
come back.

The owner was a short, round, excitable man with the wrinkles and quavering voice of a person in his seventies and with

black, black hair that we kept trying to figure if it was a toupee or not, and if it was, how we could snatch if off.

For all his wrinkles though, he could rush up and down the aisles and grap an unruly kid by the collar and march him out like nothing you ever saw. So fast that we nicknamed him Flash Gordo. We would explode into fits of laughter when one of us saw him zoom down the aisle and whispered "Flash Gordo" to the rest of us. He gave us almost as many laughs as Chris-Pin Martín of the movies.

I counted out my money that first Saturday. I was nervous, knowing what I had to do, and the pennies kept sticking to my sweaty fingers. Finally, in exasperation, Flash Gordo's long-nosed wife counted them herself, watching me like a hawk so I wouldn't try to sneak in until she got to ten, and then she growled, "All right!"

Zoom! Past the candy counter and down the aisle like I said, looking for Flash. I didn't see him until I got right up front, my heart pounding, and started to move toward the door. That's when this circular shadow loomed in the semidark, and I looked up in fright to see him standing at the edge of the stage looking at the screen. Then he turned abruptly and scowled at me as if he could read my mind. I slipped into an aisle seat and pretended I was testing it by bouncing up and down a couple of times and then sliding over to try the next one.

I thought Flash was going to say something as he walked in my direction. But he suddenly bobbed down and picked something off the floor—a dead rat?—when a yell came from the back of the theatre. "Lupe and Carlos are doing it again! Back in the last row!"

Flash bolted upright so quickly my mouth fell open. Before I could close it, he rushed up the aisle out of sight toward those sex maniacs in the last row. Of all the things Flash Gordo could not tolerate, this was the worst. And every Saturday some clown would tattle on Lupe and Carlos, and Flash would rush across the theatre. Only later did I learn that there never was any Lupe or Carlos. If there had been, I'm sure Los Indios would have kept very quiet and watched whatever it was they were doing back there.

"Oh, Carlos!" someone yelled in a falsetto. "Stop that this minute!"

I jumped out of my seat and rushed to the door to let Los Indios in. By the time Flash Gordo had shined his flashlight over and under the seats in the back, we were all across the theatre at the edge of the crowd where we wouldn't be conspicuous. Later we moved to our favorite spot in the front row where we craned our necks to look up at the giant figures acting out their adventures.

While the movies were fantastic—the highlight of our week— sometimes I think we had almost as much fun talking about them afterwards and acting them out. It was like much later when I went to high school; rehashing the Saturday night dance or party was sometimes better than the actual event.

We all had our favorites and our definite point of view about Hollywood movies. We barely tolerated those cowboy movies with actors like Johnny Mack Brown and "Wild Bill" Elliot and Gene Autry and even Hopalong Cassidy. ¡Gringos! we'd sniff with disdain. But we'd watch them in preference to roaming the streets, and we'd cheer for the Indians and sometimes for the bad guys if they were swarthy and Mexican.

They showed the Zorro movies several times each, including the serials with one chapter each Saturday. Zorro drew mixed reviews and was the subject of endless argument. "Spanish dandy!" one would scoff. "¿Dónde están los mejicanos?" Over in the background hanging onto their straw sombreros and smiling fearfully as they bowed to the tax collector, I remember.

"But at least Zorro speaks the right language."

Then somebody would hoot, "Yeah. Hollywood inglés. Look at the actors who play Zorro. Gringos every one. John Carroll. Reed Handley. Tyrone Power. ¡Mierda!"

That was what Zorro did to us. Better than Gene Autry but still a phony Spaniard while all the indios y mestizos were bit players.

That was no doubt the reason why our favorite was the Cisco Kid. Even the one gringo who played the role, Warner Baxter, could have passed for a Mexican. More than one kid said he looked like my old man, so I was one of those who accepted Warner Baxter. Somebody even thought that he was Mexican but had changed his name so he could get parts in Hollywood— you know how Hollywood is. But we conveniently leaped from that to cheering for the "real" Cisco Kids without wondering how *they* ever got parts in that Hollywood: Gilbert Roland, César Romero, Duncan Renaldo. With the arch-sidekick of all time, Chris-Pin Martín, who was better any day than Fuzzy Knight, Smiley Burnette, or Gabby Hayes.

"Sí, Ceesco," we'd lisp to each other and laugh, trying to sound like Chris-Pin.

We'd leave the theatre laughing and chattering, bumping and elbowing each other past the lobby. There Flash Gordo would stare at us as if trying to remember whether or not we had bought tickets, thoughtfully clicking his false teeth like castanets. We'd quiet down as we filed past, looking at that toupee of his that was, on closer inspection, old hair blackened with shoe polish that looked like dyed rat fur. Hasta la vista, Flash, I'd think. See you again next week.

One Saturday afternoon when I returned home there was a beat-up old truck parked in front of the empty house next door and a slow parade in and out. In the distance I saw the curious stare of a towhead about my age.

When I rushed into the house, my three-year old brother ran up to me and excitedly told me in baby-talk, "La huera. La huera, huera."

"Hush," Mama said.

Uncle Tito, who was Mama's unmarried younger brother, winked at me. "Blondie's wearing a halter top and shorts," he said. "In the back yard next door."

"Hush," Mama said to him, scowling, and he winked at me again.

That night when I was supposed to be sleeping, I heard Mama and Papa arguing. "Well," Mama said. "What do you think about that? They swept up the gutters of Oklahoma City. What was too lightweight to settle got blown across the panhandle to New Mexico. Right next door."

"Now, Josefa," Papa said. "You have to give people a chance."

"Halter top and shorts," Mama snipped. "What will the children think?"

"The only child who's going to notice is Tito, and he's old enough although sometimes he doesn't act it."

But then my eyelids started to get heavy, and the words turned into a fuzzy murmur.

One day after school that next week, Chango decided that we

needed some new adventures. We took the long way home all the
way past Fourth Street Elementary School where all the pagan
Protestants went. "Only Catholics go to heaven," Sister Mary
Margaret warned us. "Good Catholics." While her cold eye
sought out a few of us and chilled our hearts with her stare.

But after school the thaw set in. We wanted to see what those
candidates for hell looked like—those condemned souls who
attended public school. And I wondered if God had only one
spot left in heaven, and He had to choose between a bad Catholic
who spoke Spanish and a good Protestant who spoke English,
which one He would let in. A fearful possibility crossed my
mind, but I quickly dismissed it.

We rambled along picking up rocks and throwing them at
tree trunks, looking for lizards or maybe even a lost coin dulled
by weather and dirt but still very spendable. What we found was
nothing. The schoolyard was empty, so we turned back toward
home. It was then, in the large empty field across from the Río
Valley Creamery that we saw this laggard, my new neighbor, the
undesirable Okie.

Chango gave a shout of joy. There he was. The enemy. Let's
go get him! We saddled our imaginary horses and galloped into
the sunset. Meanwhile, John Wayne, which was the name I called
him then, turned his flour-white face and blinked his watery pale
eyes at us in fear. Then he took off across the field in a dead run
which only increased our excitement as if it was an admission
that he truly was the enemy and deserved thrashing.

He escaped that day, but not before he got a good look at us. I
forgot what we called him besides Okie gabacho gringo cabrón.
In my memory he was John Wayne to our Cisco Kid, maybe
because of the movie about the Alamo.

That then became our favorite after school pastime. We'd
make our way toward the Fourth Street Elementary School looking for our enemy, John Wayne. As cunning as enemies usually
are, we figured that he'd be on the lookout so we stalked him
Indian style. We missed him the next day, but the day after that
when we were still a long block away, he suddenly stopped and
lifted his head like a wild deer and seemed to feel or scent alien
vibrations in the air, because he set off at a dog trot toward
home.

"Head him off at the pass!" Chango Cisco shouted, and we

headed across toward Fifth Street. But John Wayne ran too fast, so we finally stopped and cut across to Lomas Park to work out a better plan.

We ambushed him the next day. Four of us came around the way he'd expect us to, while the other two of us sneaked the back way to intercept him between home and the elementary school. At the first sight of the stalkers he ran through the open field that was too big to be called a city lot. Chango and I waited for him behind the tamaracks. When he came near, breathing so heavily we could hear his wheeze, and casting quick glances over his shoulder, we stepped out from behind the trees.

He stopped dead. I couldn't believe anyone could stop that fast. No slow down, no gradual transition. One instant he was running full speed; the next instant he was absolutely immobile, staring at us with fright.

"You!" he said breathlessly, staring straight into my eyes.

"You!" I answered.

"¿Que hablas español?" Chango asked.

His look of fear deepened, swept now with perplexity like a ripple across the surface of water. When he didn't answer, Chango whooped out a laugh of joy and charged with clenched fists. It wasn't much of a fight. A couple of punches and a bloody nose and John Wayne was down. When we heard the shouts from the others, Chango turned and yelled to them. That was when John Wayne made his escape. We didn't follow this time. It wasn't worth it. There was no fight in him, and we didn't beat up on sissies or girls.

On the way home it suddenly struck me that, since he lived next door, he would tell his mother who might tell my mother, who would unquestionably tell my father. I entered the house with apprehension. Whether it was fear or conscience didn't matter.

But luck was with me. That night, although I watched my father's piercing looks across the dinner table with foreboding (Or was it my conscience that saw his looks as piercing?), nothing came of it. Not a word. Only questions about school. What were they teaching us to read and write in English? Were we already preparing for our First Communion? Wouldn't Grandma be proud when we went to the country next Sunday. I could read for her from my schoolbook, *Bible Stories for Children*. Only my overambitious father forgot that *Bible Stories for Children* was a third grade book that he had bought for me at a church rummage sale. I was barely at the reading level of "Run, Spot. Run." Hardly exciting fare even for my blind grandmother who spoke no English and read nothing at all.

Before Sunday though, there was Saturday. In order to do my share of the family chores and "earn" movie money instead of accepting charity, my father had me pick up in the back yard. I gathered toys that belonged to my little sister and brother, carried a bag of garbage to the heavy galvanized can out back by the shed, even helped pull a few weeds in the vegetable garden. This last was the "country" that my father carried with him to every house we lived in until I grew up and left home. You can take the boy out of the country, as the old saying goes. And in his case it was true.

I dragged my feet reluctantly out to the tiny patch of yard behind the doll's house in which we lived, ignoring my mother's scolding about not wearing out the toes of my shoes.

I must have been staring at the rubber tips of my tennis shoes to watch them wear down, so I didn't see my arch-enemy across the low fence. I heard him first. A kind of cowardly snivel that jolted me like an electric shock. Without looking I knew who it was.

"You!" he said as I looked across the fence.

"You!" I answered back with hostility.

Then his eyes watered up and his lips twitched in readiness for the blubbering that, in disgust, I anticipated.

"You hate me," he accused. I squatted down to pick up a rock, not taking my eyes off him. "Because I don't speak Spanish and I have yellow hair."

No, I thought, I don't like you because you're a sniveler. I wanted to leap the fence and punch him on those twitching lips, but I sensed my father behind me watching. Or was it my conscience again? I didn't dare turn and look.

"I hate Okies," I said. To my delight it was as if my itching fist had connected. He all but yelped in pain, though what I heard was a sharp expulsion of air.

"Denver?" The soft, feminine voice startled me, and I looked toward the back stoop of their house. I didn't see what Tito had made such a fuss about. She was blonde and pale as her son and kind of lumpy, I thought, even in the everyday house dress she wore. She tried to smile—a weak, sniveling motion of her mouth that told me how Denver had come by that same expression. Then she stepped into the yard where we boys stared at each other like tomcats at bay.

"Howdy," she said in a soft funny accent that I figured must be Oklahoma. "I was telling your mother that you boys ought to get together being neighbors and all. Denver's in the second grade at the public school."

Denver backed away from the fence and nestled against his mother's side. Before I could answer that Immaculate Heart boys didn't play with sniveling heathens, I heard our back door squeak open, then slam shut.

"I understand there's a nice movie in town where the boys go Saturday afternoons," she went on. But she was looking over my head toward whomever had come out of the house.

I looked back and saw Mama. Through the window over the kitchen sink I saw Papa. He's making sure she and I behave, I thought.

"It would be nice for the boys to go together," Mama said. She came down the steps and across the yard.

You didn't ask me! my silent angry self screamed. It's not fair! You didn't ask me! But Mama didn't even look at me; she addressed herself to Mrs. Oklahoma as if Snivel Nose and I weren't even there.

Then an unbelievable thought occurred to me. For some reason Denver had not told his mama about being chased home from school. Or if he did, he hadn't mentioned me. He was too afraid, I decided. He knew what would happen if he squealed. But even that left me with an uneasy feeling. I looked at him to see if the answer was on his face. All I got was a weak twitch of a smile and a blink of his pleading eyes.

I was struck dumb by the entire negotiation. It was settled without my comment or consent, like watching someone bargain away my life. When I went back into the house, all of my pent-up anger exploded. I screamed and kicked my heels and even cried—but to no avail.

"You have two choices, young man," my father warned. "Go

to the matinee with Denver or stay in your room." But his ominous tone of voice told me that there was another choice: a good
belting on the rear end.

Of course, this Saturday the Rat House was showing a movie
about one of our favorite subjects where the mejicanos whipped
the gringos: the Alamo. I had to go. Los Indios were counting on
me to let them in.

I walked the few blocks to town, a boy torn apart. One of me
hurried eagerly toward the Saturday afternoon adventure. The
other dragged his feet, scuffing the toes of his shoes to spite his
parents, all the while conscious of this hated stranger walking
silently beside him.

When we came within sight of the theatre, I felt Denver tense
and slow his pace even more than mine. "Your gang is waiting,"
he said, and I swear he started to tremble.

What a chicken, I thought. "You're with me," I said. But then
he had reminded me. What would I tell Chango and the rest of
Los Indios?

They came at us with a rush. "What's he doing here?"
Chango snarled.

I tried to explain. They deflected my words and listened
instead to the silent fear they heard as they scrutinized Denver.
My explanation did not wash so I tried something in despera-
tion.

"He's not what you think," I said. Scepticism and disbelief.
"Just because he doesn't understand Spanish doesn't mean he
can't be one of us." Show me! Chango's expression said. "He's—
he's—," my voice was so loud that a passerby turned and stared.
"He's an Indian from Oklahoma," I lied.

"A blond Indian?" They all laughed.

My capacity for lying ballooned in proportion to their disbelief. I grew indignant, angry, self-righteous. "Yes!" I shouted.
"An albino Indian!"

The laughs froze in their throats, and they looked at each
other, seeing their own doubts mirrored in their friends' eyes.
"Honest to God?" Chango asked.

"Honest to God!"

"Does he have money?"

Denver unfolded a sweaty fist to show the dime in his palm.
Chango took it quickly, like a rooster pecking a kernal of corn.

"Run to the dime store," he commanded the fastest of his lack-eys. "Get that hard candy that lasts a long time. And hurry. We'll meet you in the back."

Denver's mouth fell open but not a sound emerged. "When we see him running back," Chango said to me, "you buy the ticket and let us in." Then he riveted his suspicious eyes on Denver and said, "Talk Indian."

I don't remember what kind of gibberish Denver faked. It didn't have to be much because our runner had dashed across the street and down the block and was already sprinting back.

Our seven-for-the-price-of-one worked as always. When the theatre was dark, we moved to our favorite seats. In the mean-time, I had drawn Denver aside and maliciously told him he had better learn some Spanish. When we came to the crucial part of the movie he had to shout what I told him.

It was a memorable Saturday. The hard sugar candy lasted through two cartoons and half of the first feature. We relived the story of the Alamo again—we had seen this movie at least twice before, and we had seen other versions more times than I can remember. When the crucial, climactic attack began, we started our chant. I elbowed Denver to shout what I had taught him.

"¡Maten los gringos!" Kill the gringos! Then others in the audience took up the chant, while Flash Gordo ran around in circles trying to shush us up.

I sat in secret pleasure, a conqueror of two worlds. To my left was this blond Indian shouting heresies he little dreamed of, while I was already at least as proficient in English as he. On my right were my fellow tribesmen who had accepted my audacious lie and welcomed this albino redskin into our group.

But memory plays its little tricks. Years later, when I couldn't think of Denver's name, I would always remember the Alamo—and John Wayne. There were probably three or four movies about that infamous mission, but John Wayne's was the one that stuck in my mind. Imagine my shock when I learned that his movie had not been made until 1960, by which time I was al-ready through high school, had two years of college, and had gone to work. There was no way we could have seen the John Wayne version when I was in the first grade.

Looking back, I realized that Wayne, as America's gringo hero, was forever to me the bigoted Indian hater of "The

Searchers" fused with the deserving victim of the attacking Mexican forces at the Alamo—the natural enemy of the Cisco Kid.

Another of my illusions shattered hard when I later learned that in real life Wayne had married a woman named Pilar or Chata or maybe both. That separated the man, the actor, from the characters he portrayed and left me in total confusion.

But then life was never guaranteed to be simple. For I saw the beak of the chick I was at six years old pecking through the hard shell of my own preconceptions. Moving into an alien land. First hating, then becoming friends with aliens like my blond Indian Okie friend, Denver, and finally becoming almost an alien myself.

El Patrón

My father-in-law's hierarchy is, in descending order: Dios, El Papa, y el patrón. It is to these that mere mortals bow, as in turn el patrón bows to El Papa, and El Papa bows to Dios.

God and the Pope are understandable enough. It's this el patrón, the boss, who causes most of our trouble. Whether it's the one who gives you work and for it pay, the lifeblood of hardworking little people, or others: our parents (fathers affectionately known as "jefe," mothers known merely as "Mamá"), military commanders ("el capitán"), or any of the big shots in the government ("el alcalde," el gobernador," "el presidente," and never forget "la policía"). It was about some such el patrón trouble that Señor Martínez boarded the bus in San Diego and headed north toward L.A.—and us.

Since I was lecturing to a midafternoon summer school class at Southwestern U, my wife Lola picked up her father at the station. When I arrived home, they were sitting politely in the living room talking banalities: "Yes, it does look like rain. But if it doesn't rain, it might be sunny. If only the clouds would blow away."

Lola had that dangerous look on her face that made me start talking too fast and too long in hope of shifting her focus. It never worked. She'd sit there with a face like a brown-skinned kewpie doll whose expression was slowly turning into that of an angry maniac. When she could no longer stand it, she'd give her father a blast: "You never talk to me about anything important, you macho, chauvinist jumping bean!" Then it would escalate to nastiness from there.

But tonight it didn't get that far. As I entered, Señor Martínez rose, dressed in his one suit as for a wedding or a funeral, and politely shook my hand. Without so much as a glance at Lola he said, "Why don't you go to the kitchen with the other women."

"There are no other women," Lola said coldly. She stood and belligerently received my kiss on the cheek before leaving.

Señor Martínez was oblivious to her reaction, sensing only the absence of "woman," at which he visibly relaxed.

"Rosca," he said, referring to me as he always did by my last name. "Tito is in trouble with the law."

His face struggled between anger and sadness, tinged with a crosscurrent of confusion. Tito was his pride and joy. His only son after four daughters. A twilight gift born to his wife at a time when he despaired of ever having a son, when their youngest daughter Lola was already ten years old and their oldest daughter twenty.

"He just finished his examinations at the state university. He was working this summer to save money for his second year when this terrible thing happened."

I could not in my wildest fantasies imagine young Vicente getting into trouble. He impressed me as a bright, polite young man who would inspire pride in any father. Even when he and old Vicente had quarreled about Tito going to college instead of working full time, the old man had grudgingly come around to seeing the wisdom of it. But now. The law! I was stunned.

"Where is he?" I asked, imagining the nineteen-year old in some filthy cell in the San Diego jail.

"I don't know." Then he looked over his shoulder toward the kitchen as if to be certain no one was eavesdropping. "I think he went underground."

Underground! I had visions of drug crazed revolutionary zealots. Bombs exploding in Federal Buildings. God knows what kind of madness.

"They're probably after him," he went on. Then he paused and stared at me as if trying to understand. "Tito always looked up to you and Lola. Of all the family it would be you he would try to contact. I want you to help me." Not help Tito, I thought, but help *me*.

I went to the cabinet and poured from the bottle that I keep for emergencies. I took a swallow to give me courage to ask the question. "What . . . did . . . he do?"

Señor Martínez stared limply at the glass in his hand. "You know," he said, "my father fought with Pancho Villa."

Jesus! I thought. If everyone who told me his father had fought with Pancho Villa was telling the truth, that army would have been big enough to conquer the world. Besides—what did this have to do with Tito?

"When my turn came," he continued, "I enlisted in the Marines at Camp Pendleton. Fought los japoneses in the Pacific." Finally he took a sip of his drink and sat stiffly as if at attention. "The men in our family have never shirked their duty!" He barked like the Marine corporal he had once been.

It slowly dawned on me what this was all about. It had been *the* topic during summer school at Southwestern U. Registration for the draft. "No blood for mideast oil!" the picket signs around the campus post office had shouted. "Boycott the Exxon army!"

"I should never have let him go to college," Señor Martínez said. "That's where he gets such crazy radical ideas. From those rich college boys whose parents can buy them out of all kinds of trouble."

"So he didn't register," I said.

"The FBI is probably after him right now. It's a Federal crime, you know. And the Canadians don't want draft dodgers either."

He took a deep swallow, polishing off the rest of his drink, and put the empty glass on the coffee table. There, his gesture seemed to say, now you know the worst.

Calmer now, he went on to tell me more. About the American Civil War; a greater percentage of Spanish-speaking men of New Mexico had joined the Union Army than the men from any other group in any other state. About the Rough Riders, including young Mexican-Americans, born on horseback, riding roughest of all over the Spanish in Cuba. About the War-to-End-All-Wars, where tough, skinny, brown-faced doughboys from farms in Texas, New Mexico, Arizona, Colorado, and California gave their all "Over There." About World War II, from the New Mexico National Guard captured at Bataan to the tough little Marines whom he was proud to fight alongside; man for man there were more decorations for bravery among Mexican-Americans than among any other group. Then Korea, where his younger brother toughed it out in the infantry. Finally Vietnam, where kids like his nephew, Pablo, got it in some silent, dark jungle trying to save a small country from the Communists.

By now he had lost his calm. There were tears in his eyes, partly from the pride he felt in this tradition of valor. But partly for something else, I thought. I could almost hear his son's reply to his impassioned call to duty: "Yes, Papá. So we could come back, if we survive, to our jobs as busboys and ditch diggers; that's why I have to go to college. I don't want to go to the Middle East and fight and die for some oil company when you can't even afford to own a car. If the Russians invaded our country, I would defend it. If a robber broke into our house, I would fight him. If someone attacked you, I would save you. But this? No, Papá."

But now Tito was gone. God knows where. None of his three sisters in San Diego had seen him. Nor any of his friends in the neighborhood or school or work.

I could hear preparations for dinner from the kitchen. Señor Martínez and I had another traguito while Lolita and Junior ate their dinner early, the sounds of their childish voices piercing through the banging of pots and pans.

When Lola called me Emiliano instead of by my nickname, Pata, I knew we were in for a lousy meal. Everything her father disliked must have been served. It had taken a perverse gourmet expending a tremendous amount of energy to fix such rotten food. There was that nothing white bread that presses together into a doughy flat mess instead of the tortillas Papá thrived on. There was a funny little salad with chopped garbage in it covered by a blob of imitation goo. There was no meat. *No meat!* Just all those sliced vegetables in a big bowl. Not ordinary vegetables like beans and potatoes and carrots, but funny, wiggly long things like wild grass—or worms. And quivering cubes of what must have been whale blubber. But enough. You get the idea.

Halfway through the meal, as Señor Martínez shuffled the food around on his plate like one of our kids resisting what was good for them, the doorbell rang.

"You'd better get that, Emiliano," Lola said, daring me to refuse by her tone of voice and dagger-throwing glance.

Who needs a fight? In a sense I was lucky because I could leave the table and that pot of mess-age. When I opened the door, a scraggly young man beamed at me. "I hitchhiked from San Diego," Tito said.

Before I could move onto the steps and close the door behind me, he stumbled past into the house. Tired as he was, he reacted instantly to seeing his father at the table. "You!" he shouted, then turned and bolted out the door.

Even tired he could run faster than me, so I hopped into the car and drove after him while Lola and Señor Martínez stood on the steps shouting words I couldn't hear.

Two blocks later Tito climbed into the car when I bribed him with a promise of dinner at McDonald's. While his mouth was full I tried to talk some sense into him, but to no avail. He was just as stubborn as his father and sister. Finally, I drove him to the International House on campus where the housing manager, who owed me a favor, found him an empty bed.

"You should have made him come back with you," Lola nagged at me that night.

"He doesn't want to be under the same roof with his father." From her thoughtful silence I knew that she understood and felt the same way. When I explained to her what it was all about—her father had said nothing to her—it looked for a moment as if she would get out of bed, stomp to the guest room, and heave Señor Martínez out into the street.

The next day was an endless two-way shuttle between our house and the I House. First me. Then Lola. If Señor Martínez had had a car and could drive, he would have followed each of us.

Our shuttle diplomacy finally wore them down. At last there were cracks in father's and son's immovable positions.

"Yes. Yes. I love my son."

"I love my father."

"I know. I know. Adults should be able to sit down and talk about their differences, no matter how wrong he is."

"Maybe tomorrow. Give me a break. But definitely not at mealtime. I can't eat while my stomach is churning."

The difficulty for me, as always, was in keeping my opinions to myself. Lola didn't have that problem. After all, they were her brother and father, so she felt free to say whatever she pleased.

"The plan is to get them to talk," I said to her. "If they can talk, they can reach some kind of understanding."

"Papá has to be set straight," she said. "As usual, he's wrong, but he always insists it's someone else who messed things up."

"He doesn't want Tito to go to jail."

"That's Tito's choice!" Of course she was right; they were both right.

The summit meeting was set for the next afternoon. Since I had only one late morning lecture, I would pick up Tito, feed him a Big Mac or two, then bring him to the house. Lola would fix Señor Martínez some nice tortillas and chili, making up for that abominable dinner of the night before last. Well fed, with two chaperones mediating, we thought they could work something out.

When Tito and I walked into the house, hope started to tremble and develop goose bumps. It was deathly silent and formal. Lola had that dangerous look on her face again. The macho, chauvinist jumping bean sat stiffly in his suit that looked like it had just been pressed—all shiny and sharply creased, unapproachable and potentially cutting, warning of what lay behind Señor Martínez's stone face.

Tito and I sat across from the sofa and faced them. Or rather I faced them. Both Tito and Señor Martínez were looking off at an angle from each other, not daring to touch glances. I smiled, but no one acknowledged it so I gave it up. Then Lola broke the silence.

"What this needs is a woman's point-of-view," she began.

That's all Señor Martínez needed. The blast his eyes shot at her left her open-mouthed and silent as he interrupted. "I don't want you to go to jail!" He was looking at Lola, but he meant Tito.

Tito's response was barely audible, and I detected a trembling in his voice. "You'd rather I got killed on some Arabian desert."

The stone face cracked. For a moment it looked as if Señor Martínez would burst into tears. He turned his puzzled face from Lola toward his son. "No," he said. "Is that what you think?" Then, when Tito did not answer, he said, "You're my only son. Damn it! Sons are supposed to obey their fathers!"

"El patrón, El Papa, and Dios," Tito said with a trace of bitterness.

But Lola could be denied no longer. "Papá, how old were you when you left Mexico for the U.S.?" She didn't expect an answer, so didn't give him time to reply. "Sixteen, wasn't it? And what did your father say?"

Thank God that smart-ass smile of hers was turned away from her father. She knew she had him, and he knew it too, but he didn't need her smirk to remind him.

He sighed. The look on his face showed that sometimes memories were best forgotten. He shook his head but did not speak. Lola had seen her father's reaction, and her voice lost its hard edge and became more sympathetic.

"He disowned you, didn't he? Grandpa disowned you. Called you a traitor to your own country. A deserter when things got tough."

"I did not intend to stay in Mexico and starve," he said. He looked around at us one by one as if he had to justify himself. "He eventually came to Los Estados Unidos himself. He and Mamá died in that house in San Diego."

"What did you think when Grandpa did that to you?"

No answer was necessary. "Can't you see, Papá?" Lola pleaded.

Meanwhile Tito had been watching his father as if he had never seen him before. Only the older children had heard Papá's story of how he left Mexico.

"I don't intend to go to jail, Papá," Tito said. "I just have to take a stand along with thousands of others. In the past old men started wars in which young men died in order to preserve old men's comforts. It just has to stop.

"There's never been a war without a draft. Never a draft without registration. And this one is nothing but craziness by el patrón in Washington, D.C. If enough of us protest, maybe he'll get the message."

"They almost declared it unconstitutional," I said. "They may yet."

"Because they aren't signing women," Papá said in disgust. But from the look on Lola's face, I'd pick her over him in any war.

"If they come after me, I'll register," Tito said. "But in the meantime I have to take this stand."

There. It was out. They had had their talk in spite of their disagreements.

"He's nineteen," Lola said. "Old enough to run his own life."

Señor Martínez was all talked out. He slumped against the back of the sofa. Even the creases in his trousers sagged. Tito looked at his sister, and his face brightened.

"Papá," Tito said. "I—I'd like to go home if you want me to."

On Papá's puzzled face I imagined I could see the words: "My father fought with Pancho Villa." But it was no longer an accusation, only a simple statement of fact. Who knows what takes more courage: to fight or not to fight?

"There's a bus at four o'clock," Señor Martínez said.

Later I drove them in silence to the station. Though it was awkward, it wasn't a bad silence. There are more important ways to speak than with words, and I could feel that sitting shoulder to shoulder, father and son had reached some accord.

Papá still believed in el patrón, El Papa, and Dios. What I hoped they now saw was that Tito did too. Only in his case, conscience overrode el patrón, maybe even El Papa. In times past, Popes too declared holy wars that violated conscience. For Tito, conscience was the same as Dios. And I saw, in their uneasy truce, that love overrode their differences.

I shook their hands as they boarded the bus, and watched the two similar faces, one old, one young, smile sadly at me through the window as the Greyhound pulled away.

When I got back home, Junior and Lolita were squabbling over what channel to watch on TV. I rolled my eyes in exasperation, ready to holler, but Lola spoke first.

"I'm glad Papá got straightened out. The hardest thing for parents is to let go of their children."

Yeah, I started to say, but she stuck her head into the den and shouted at Junior and Lolita to stop quarreling or they were going to get it.

Nouvelle Cuisine

Although it would soon be the week of final exams, I would have gladly sold my textbooks to raise money to take Matilde Ríos to dinner. Never mind that it was the critical last year of my graduate career. All that was left were a few courses, the final touches on my thesis, then with luck, on to teaching or research with a brand new PhD clutched tightly in my hand. But Matilde Ríos made me forget the three years of graduate study with its long, late hours, its diplomatic conferences with a graduate advisor who was more intellectual robot than human being, and the ragged edge of poverty while friends who had forsaken graduate school were flashing around in their Datsun 280 Z's and well-tailored cashmere jackets.

The waiter led us to the table, handed us menus, and told us that his name was Andre. As he went off, Matilde's eyes raised discreetly from the menu and looked around at the lack of decor that did not go with the absence of prices.

Her reddish-brown hair fell softly to her shoulders, and her skin was the color of rich cream, not what you'd normally expect in a girl from Central America. When she turned her light brown eyes with flecks of gold toward me, my knees melted and my hands trembled.

"It's the chef," I explained. "It's the food that counts here, not the atmosphere."

Her lips parted in a tiny smile as she nodded. The blue bruise on her left temple was barely visible under the skillfully applied makeup, and the swelling had receded.

"Do you speak Spanish?" she asked in her whisper of a voice. It was tinged with the slightest of accents that brought to mind Mata Hari engaged on a dangerous mission.

I shook my head. "I understand a little. My mother is a Texican. Her maiden name was Morales. My father met her in San Antonio when he was in the Air Force. He's just plain old Irish-American. That's how I came out Kevin Reilly-Morales."

She looked at the menu again. "It's too expensive," she said as her eyes moved down and across, conjuring numbers in the white spaces alongside the offerings. There was judgement in her voice, a sense that such capitalistic decadence was immoral in the light of hunger and poverty in so much of the world.

My ears flamed. "It's my twenty-fifth birthday. My parents sent me a check."

Now the brown-gold eyes stared intently. "But you should save it for something special." I didn't want to tell her that I had.

While she studied the menu, I watched her, returning to the bruise that had been the reason we had met and were here tonight on our first date. I had just finished a late breakfast at the Dining Commons on campus last Tuesday and was on my way to a conference with my graduate advisor. I was early for a change, so I lingered over a second cup of coffee before setting off for the Physics Department.

When I left the Commons, a line of picketers slowly made its way along Sproul Plaza toward Sather Gate. I hardly paid attention to it. It was a common enough occurrence at Berkeley, and this march was pretty mild compared to many. All that distinguished it from the everyday flood of students hurrying from Telegraph Avenue onto campus were its deliberate pace and the signs sticking above the crowd like the disconnected vertebrae of a long, human snake.

Suddenly a shout catalyzed the crowd. I was already in the thick of the mob, waiting for the picketers to pass so I could cross to the east side of the plaza. There was a rush from the left of Sather Gate. Signs were thrown to the ground while others were swung at the attackers.

It was then that I heard Spanish curses, and I turned toward the scuffle on my left. A sign wavered in a struggle of grappling hands: "¡Venceremos!" it read. "¡Libertad por El Salvador!" "Victory will be ours! Liberty for El Salvador!"

I didn't see who shoved me. When I turned to defend myself, the sign had been ripped from the hands of a young woman who was shouting at an attacker with his back toward her. He turned and struck her on the side of the head with the sign. I was torn between hitting him and helping her. When she fell to the walk and the mob surged, starting to stampede, I bent over and lifted her in my arms, pushing and shoving my way through the crowd. Semiconscious, she bled onto the front of my good wool sweater as I carried her to the steps of Sproul Hall. I stopped to catch my breath and figure out what to do next. The picketers had been driven away. I felt her stir against my breast. "Take me home," she said in Spanish.

It was an ugly bruise, and I had a desperate feeling that a doctor's office or emergency hospital would be better. But she insisted again as she let go of me and tried to get to her feet. The wail of police sirens made the choice for us. I led her toward the parking structure by the tennis courts and drove to the old house in Berkeley that she shared with five other coeds.

"May I bring you something from the bar?" Andre had returned. I ordered a bottle of California wine. He came back quickly, cradling the bottle in both hands, label up, so we could see. Then he put his cork puller to work and poured me a sample. After he filled our glasses, he took our orders. There were two entrees as there were here every night. It was pasta with lobster and asparagus for Matilde, and for me, charcoal-grilled quail with shallots and parsley.

Matilde winced when I ordered, but I didn't think anything of it. We sipped our wine, a delicious chenin blanc, ate the fresh salad of homegrown greens with vinaigrette, and I talked of inconsequentials, trying to draw her out of her reserve.

"So," she finally said. "You're studying physics? What is it that people do with physics, besides make bombs?"

Oh, oh, I thought. "I'm writing my thesis on materials research. The effects of impurities on electronic phenomena. You know. Like silicon used in semiconductors and microprocessors, that sort of thing."

She nodded, but her face was a blank. I sensed that she hadn't really heard me. "And you like . . . little birds?" she asked. "Quail?"

Her solemn, judgmental attitude was beginning to annoy me. Sure, I thought. And you like little fish . . . lobster. But I just smiled, trying to puzzle through the beautiful exterior to something underneath that I couldn't see or understand.

"You're in Latin American Studies," I said. "What are you going to do with that, teach?"

She shrugged and gave me a smile that was not so much heartfelt as a dismissal of the question. Woman of mystery, I thought, what are you hiding?

"How long have you been in the U.S.?" I asked.

Some part of her came alive—finally. "Nine years. My . . . parents sent me to a private girls' school in Menlo Park. Sacred Heart. Where deposed South American dictators with Swiss bank accounts send their daughters. You've heard of it?" I shook my head. "I came to the university from there. I started my graduate work this year." Her brown-gold eyes stared right through me. For a moment they moistened, and I thought she might shed a delicate tear or two, but they snapped quickly back under control like two little pedigree dogs brought to heel. "I haven't been to San Salvador in nine years."

"You should go back home for a visit."

Too late I realized what I'd said and saw her tremble with a delicate shudder. "It would be dangerous."

I waited for her to volunteer more. Instead she gave another smile of dismissal, and I went on innocuously about one of the latest movies in town. She really didn't seem to take in what I was saying, though occasionally she would ask a brief question or coo an exclamation. Then her whisper of a voice would wash over me like a warm sea breeze, her lilting accent like the pulsing of distant surf. Andre saved us from a potential fiasco—she seemed to sense that I knew she wasn't listening—when he served our entrees.

We ate in silence except for the polite chatter of silver and the not quite suppressed, gentle sounds of teeth and lips, our most successful conversation so far. Matilde did not look at me once as I devoured the little bird. She ate her pasta and lobster as if she were not hungry or was restrained by some thought that bordered on revulsion.

Only when the waiter cleared our plates did she look up. Then it was to cast a long, sad look at the remnants of tiny bones piled on my plate. She sighed, and I sensed remorse and pain peeking out from the hidden place.

Dessert was an apricot souffle that was magnificent. That and strong coffee pulled Matilde from the pit in which she had lingered much of the evening. Jesus, I thought. What a dud of a date. Then the fearful thought popped out unsolicited: Maybe it's me.

No, damn it! I thought angrily. It isn't. How could any sensible young woman that I was attracted to not reciprocate? Wasn't I a good catch? Intelligent? Enlightened? Reasonably decent looking? With a good future?

Perhaps the same thoughts were occurring to her. At any rate, dessert and coffee seemed to lighten Matilde's mood, and she was smiling now as we talked, unforced and almost heedless of whatever it was that deeply troubled her.

It was while she sipped at her second cup of coffee that I decided to meet it head on. This relationship wasn't going anywhere, much to my distress, so what the hell?

"I'm sorry you're not having a very good time," I said.

Her mask of composure gave way to a look of genuine surprise. "Why . . . it was a lovely dinner."

"It doesn't make you feel guilty because so many of your countrymen are going hungry tonight while we feast?"

Her face clouded in the closest to anger that I had seen since the disrupted march in Sproul Plaza. "The United States is now my country," she said.

"You've hardly said a word all through dinner," I said. "It surely couldn't be your convent training. You're too modern to need a dueña. At least I didn't see one with you when you were carrying a picket sign."

Her response was an angry glower that would have been more malignant if she hadn't been so beautiful. "Does your injury still bother you?" She shook her head rapidly. For an instant I thought she was going to leap to her feet and storm out of the restaurant.

"You didn't even like my entree," I went on, my irritation feeding on itself. "Not only did you pick on my poor little bird, but you wouldn't even look at it when the waiter brought it."

There were tears in her eyes. She looked miserable. Oh, Christ, I thought. What the hell's the matter with me? I reached over and put my hand on hers as two tiny pearls of tears rolled down her cheeks.

"I'm sorry," I apologized. "That was cruel of me." Once again she shook her head, sniffing at her tears, and smiled weakly. "You must think I'm just a spoiled, overprivileged American. Some poor family in El Salvador could have eaten for weeks on what our dinner cost."

"Don't give in to guilt," she said. "It's hard enough managing your own life without trying to save someone else's. This was the loveliest dinner I've had since . . . I can't remember when."

"Even my little bird?"

She shuddered, stared hard into my eyes as if trying to decide something, then finally spoke. "I—I didn't want to say anything while we were eating. But now—" Again she stared for a moment, thinking. "Let me tell you."

She nodded as Andre came with coffee, then began. "I was fourteen when I last saw my home in the city of San Salvador. What did I know about anything? We had a beautiful home in the finest part of the city, servants, a finca—that is, a coffee plantation—that was a tropical paradise, a house on the shore of the Pacific, everything one could wish for.

"It was not enough for my father. What I mean is, not enough that he had all he wanted while so many had nothing. He could not be self-satisfied the way so many of our neighbors and friends were.

"He had been in the governments of several regimes, the cabinet of two. The changes, the upheavals, the revolutions were endless, going back even to when he had been a boy. Always he had been in favor of land reform, of doing something for the poor and powerless.

"Nine years ago, just before I came to the United States, he was out of the government, swept aside in one of those endless coups that settle nothing. This time his ideas made him dangerous in the eyes of the new regime.

"My father knew the danger, but it did not stop him. He was negotiating with other groups to put pressure on the government for reform. He and my mother had travelled out of the country on such a mission. Some said to Havana, while others said Washington, D.C. At any rate, they first flew to Mexico City from where one can go anywhere in the world.

"They left me with my Aunt Consuela, my father's younger sister, and our trusted servants. There was no danger, of that they were sure. They would only be gone a few days, then return to continue their work." She stopped to sip her coffee and stare thoughtfully over my shoulder. "Only this time it was different."

Her look of sadness spoke of sorrows almost too much to bear. I did not dare ask what had happened to her parents. All sorts of horrors flashed through my mind.

"It was Pepe," she went on. "Poor little Pepe."

"Pepe?"

But it was as if she hadn't heard me, or didn't want to. "At that time my Aunt Consuela had an unwelcome suitor, Herminio Delgado. He was—how shall I say it? Far beneath her. Though an uneducated man, he had maneuvered his way in the army to the rank of major because of his ruthlessness and fawning loyalty to whomever he followed at the moment. When the political winds changed, he changed too, like a chameleon, always advancing his career.

"At that time, when he would call on my aunt, she would tell the servants to say she was out. Afterwhile he must have doubted that she still lived there or suspected that she did not want to see him. Meanwhile, of course, there was Pepe.

"Pepe was only a year old at the time. Consuela had gotten him for me as a birthday present, the most beautiful, intelligent parrot you ever saw. The two of us taught him to speak. He was so quick, so smart. We used to laugh, saying that he carried on a much better conversation than Major Delgado. And Pepe had better political sense too. I had even taught him to say '¡Viva la revolución!', thinking how clever, never dreaming of the possible consequences.

"The day after my parents left, fighting broke out in the countryside. Of course, what did I understand, a naive girl of fourteen? It meant little to me, although I sensed my aunt's alarm.

"She went out early that morning with our maid Flor. Shopping was what she told me, but she had really gone out to learn what she could about the situation. I went to the convent school as usual. When I came home at the end of the day, Consuela was still gone as were the cook and chauffeur. It did not alarm me. I played with Pepe, teaching him a song that I had just learned to pick on my guitar.

"When I heard the knock at the door, I thought that my aunt

had forgotten her key, or that one of the servants had forgotten theirs although they usually entered by the rear. 'Wait a minute, Pepe,' I said. 'I'll be right back.'

"I put down my guitar and went to the door as Pepe bid me farewell with '¡Viva la revolución!' Imagine my shock when Major Delgado stood there grim-faced, stamping his feet impatiently.

"'La Señorita Ríos,' he said.

"'She's not here.' His eyes narrowed, and he looked over my shoulder into the house, his glance shifting here and there. 'She went shopping,' I said.

"'Tell her to contact me immediately. By telephone if the telephones are still working. It's a matter of the utmost urgency.' With that he about-faced and marched hurriedly to the car that waited, motor running. The last I heard as I closed the door was Pepe screaming, '¡Viva la revolución!' Suddenly my chest ached with fear, and I looked out the window.

"'Shhh,' I warned Pepe. 'You must not say that.'

"When Consuela came home it was as if events had wound her up so that she moved and talked at double speed. She did not say anything to me except that everything would be all right, but I heard her tell Flor to pack a bag for each of us right away. Then she stared at the telephone for the longest time before she picked it up.

"'I know what he's going to say,' she told me. 'I already know.' But she did not tell me. I watched anxiously. All I could hear of her telephone conversation was, 'Yes. Of course. I understand. What's that? What time?' It could have been about anything.

"She hung up and stared thoughtfully at the telephone, a finger to the side of her mouth, when Pepe shouted his greeting from the other room. '¡Viva la revolución!' She turned suddenly and looked toward the shout, then to me, and I could see the fear on her face.

"'We're going to have guests for dinner,' she said. It was like she was talking in her sleep. Then she screamed, '¡Juanita!' and hurried to the kitchen. After a moment I followed and stood at a distance as she whispered to the cook. I was frightened. I wanted to know what was going on, what was happening to my mother and father.

"Consuela took me by the arm and led me to her room and closed the door. 'Your mother and father are safe,' she said. 'I sent a message to warn them. It would be better if they did not come back just now.' She pondered a moment, wondering no doubt how much to tell me. Only much later did I learn that my father's name was at the top of a government death list. 'The outbreak of fighting surprised and alarmed the authorities,' she continued. 'They have declared martial law—but quietly. They do not want to alarm people into joining the opposition.'

"I was upset, naturally. I would be without my dear mother and father for who knows how long. 'Major Delgado is coming for dinner,' my aunt said. 'He and his Colonel.' She nodded sternly. 'Everything must go on as normally as ever. At the proper time I want you to leave the table and go to your room. Then do what Flor tells you.'

"'How will I know the proper time?'

"'You'll know,' she said.

"'What will Flor tell me?'

"'You'll have to ask Flor. But not until the proper time. Now go and get some rest. They will be here in an hour.'

"I cried every minute of that hour. Only the firm knock on my door forced me to dry my tears. Flor came in, bossing me around as always to get ready. Our self-invited dinner guests had been very punctual.

"Consuela was dazzling that night. She was dressed as if attending the president's ball. Her smile was constant and relaxed, as if she truly meant it. I could see the Major staring at her greedily. You could almost see the saliva running down the sides of his mouth.

"Colonel Mendoza was the head of military intelligence. He was second only to the supreme military commander, which gives you some idea of the kind of army it was. He was very polite, very friendly, and seemed in awe of my father. But with those secret police types you can never tell what is or isn't real.

"Aunt Consuela was charming and flattering without being either obvious or nauseous to the extreme. I knew there was danger. Of what I wasn't sure. Throughout the soup and salad I half listened to the conversation, while another part of me was fearfully alert for some indiscreet scream from Pepe. But not a

word, not a screech. It was only after some moments of parrot
silence that I realized his cage had been empty as I had hurried
past, late to the dinner table.

"As the adults talked and ate and drank, Juanita, in a clean
uniform, brought in the entree on a silver serving dish. She
lifted the domed lid, polished so bright you could see your face
as in a mirror, for my aunt's inspection. 'Our guests,' Consuela
said. 'Serve Matilde and me from the other tray.' So Juanita went
first to the Colonel, then to the Major, serving them the beauti-
fully prepared fowl covered with a delicate sauce, before she
went back to the kitchen to bring us our chicken.

"Our guests were served the larger chicken halves. What
huge birds, I thought. When I looked at the leg and sliced breast
on my own plate, comparing it, I was shocked by a horrible
premonition. I barely heard the Colonel's soft, polite voice.

"'Delicious, Señorita Ríos. I have always heard that your
brother served the finest food in San Salvador, finer than the
most exclusive restaurant. It has the strong, tangy flavor of wild
game.' Consuela gave him a quick, grim smile as he cut another
piece and popped the huge portion into his thin-lipped mouth.

"'I feel almost indecent speaking of troubling rumors while
enjoying your hospitality,' the Colonel continued.

"Meanwhile Major Delgado was cutting furiously at his own
portion, too polite or perhaps too restrained by his commanding
officer's affability, to complain about the obviously tough bird. I
could see him chewing long after the mouthful should have been
swallowed.

"'What rumors?' my aunt asked, appearing surprised.

"The Colonel laid his fork and knife on his plate and took a
sip of wine. He raised his hands shoulder high and rotated them
delicately in a vague sort of motion. 'Unconfirmed. So many
rumors are.' Consuela smiled. 'There have been reports,' the
Colonel said, 'of outcries of sympathy for the revolutionaries
coming from this house. Perhaps a clandestine meeting? A
pledge of support—?'

"'Perhaps a drama on the radio,' Consuela said. It was the
Colonel's turn to smile.

"'These are troubled times, Señorita. Now, with the unclean
rabble in revolt, we have no choice but to destroy them . . . and
watch for signs of corruption among the rest of the populace.'

"Consuela had leaned forward to better hear the Colonel. Now she leaned back, turning her head to flick me a look that told me it was time to go. I stared from her to the Colonel's plate that was fast turning into a graveyard of small bones. Then I looked at Major Delgado whose labored chewing kept him from joining in the conversation.

"'Auntie,' I said. 'I don't feel well. Please, may I be excused?'

"I felt the glare of three pair of eyes as if they could see into my mind. 'Why, you haven't finished your dinner,' the Major protested.

"'I'm not hungry.' The dawning realization of what our guests were enjoying had filled me with an unbearable nausea, and I felt that if I didn't leave immediately, I would be sick at the table.

"'If you don't feel well, my dear,' Consuela said, 'go to your room. We are almost finished. I'm sure we have more to talk about that would not interest you.'

"The Major looked curious as I stood, excused myself, and hurried away. I hesitated, almost stopping at the empty cage in the next room, but I remembered my aunt's grim look and rushed past. Flor was waiting, coat on, her bag and mine beside the bed, my coat folded over her arm.

"The first thing she said to me was, 'It couldn't be helped.' She meant Pepe. 'Now we must leave through the back. The car is waiting.'

"I started to cry. 'My guitar,' I wailed. 'How can I live without my guitar?'

"'You can live without anything,' she said, 'except hope. Now hurry.'"

Matilde sat silent across the dinner table from me with solemn eyes. Only now did she seem to relax. She took a sip from her coffee cup, put it down—it was empty—and drank from her water glass instead. My gourmet dinner had turned to hot stone in my stomach, and I was seized by a silence that gripped my throat like a garrote.

"That was the last time I saw my home in San Salvador," Matilde said.

"But your aunt?"

"It took me a long time to forgive her for what she had done. Even after she and Juanita joined us in a village near the Guatemalan border, I was angry with her. From there we made our way to Guatemala City, then to Mexico City. We stayed with a great-uncle of mine who had been in the diplomatic corps and had sought asylum in Mexico two, three revolutions prior. As soon as she could, Consuela put me on an airplane to San Francisco to join my parents. It was only then, when we were saying goodbye, that I cried and forgave her for saving my life in such a cruel way.

"'I'm sorry about Pepe,' she said. 'But I did not want you to forget those savages who forced themselves to our table, who would have had us shot without compunction. Now you will always remember.'"

Andre came with the check, then returned with my change. As we left, the hot stone in my stomach had cooled a little.

"I have never had another pet," Matilde said. "Although I still play the guitar. If I ever do own a pet again, it will be a poisonous snake." She flashed me a dangerous smile as we went through the restaurant door.

¿Venceremos? I thought, thinking about a possible romance. Not with this chick. She took my arm and squeezed it as we walked toward the car, giving me a dizzying smile. Why was it that instead of a growing warmth in the heart and groin, instead of the kindling of lust, I felt a vague premonition that I was being marched to a firing squad?

Carnitas y huesitos

I don't remember exactly when mi tío started to have those—
what shall I call them?—premonitions? visions? hallucinations?

I used to drive across the river to the southwest edge of town
to fill my car with gas and occasionally, when the prices weren't
too high, pick up a few groceries at the mom and pop tienda he
and Tía Annie owned.

They weren't doing too well. Though none of us in the family
had enough to be philanthropists—we just barely made ends
meet ourselves—those of us who could afford cars needed to buy
gasoline somewhere so why not there? Especially since Tía was,
in my mother's words, her closest sister and a saint.

Anyway, it must have been that time when my damned car
was in the shop for a week, and I had to take the bus to work. The
city bus got my gasoline money, and the next time I drove to La
Tiendita I felt a little guilty as if somehow I had betrayed my
aunt and uncle.

Tía Annie, dressed in blue jeans, came out to the pump. It
was one of those funny old red tanks with the clear glass up top
so you could see the amber liquid sloshing around. She could
probably get a fortune for it at some antique sale.

"Tío Willie isn't feeling too good today, Sonny," she said. She
smiled in that gentle, shy way of hers. "He says it's his liver, but I
think it's his chest. Even when the doctor warned him to quit
smoking, he just said, 'You can't scare me.' You know Willie."

I peeled off a few limp, dirty singles and some loose change
and paid her. A beat-up pickup truck snorted and bucked into
the dirt drive right behind me so we didn't get to talk. But I saw a
head in the window of the store, a large, hairy, ghostly head like
death eating a stale tortilla. Then a hand came into view and
beckoned to me.

I pulled over beside the building to make room for the pickup, and Tío Willie stuck his head out the door and beckoned once more. He winked and made a fist with his thumb upright like the neck of a bottle and pantomimed taking a drink. Well, I thought, there go today's profits. Tío's going to treat me to a beer.

I went into the little adobe building with neatly stacked shelves. The smell of fresh vegetables reminded me of those roadside stands you used to see in the country when I was a kid.

Willie went over to the cooler and pulled out a bottle of Coors. He opened it with the metal key attached by a tarnished chain to the cash register and handed it to me. Surprise! For the first time I could remember Tío was not joining in.

He leaned forward, almost nose to nose. "I heard her last night," he said. "Down by the river."

"Heard who?" I asked.

"La Llorona." The Weeper. Sure. Yeah. Uh-huh, I thought.

He must have seen something in my face because he put a hand on my arm and said, "Honest to God."

"You couldn't have," I said. "She's an old country superstition, and the immigration people stop her at the border. She doesn't have papers."

But Tío wasn't about to be joshed out of this foolishness. His face settled into an even more serious expression. "Tío," I went on, "people around here haven't heard La Llorona for a hundred years. This is Los Estados Unidos. Urban U.S. *New* Mexico, not *Old* Mexico."

His look was suspicious now, like I was some kind of loon. "She came back," he insisted, "and she had papers."

Well, what are you going to do? I still had half a bottle of beer. "What did she say?" I asked.

He answered solemnly, as if confiding matters of state or a pronunciamento from the Pope. "The price of gasoline is going up."

"I could have told you that, Tío. And I could cry about it, too."

"She told me to get ready. I'm going to be lifted bodily into heaven. I'm fasting for forty days and forty nights in preparation. This is the tenth day. All I take is a little water. The grace of God is food enough for me."

Well, I chugalugged the rest of that bottle and banged it onto the counter. As I turned to ease my way out, he caught me by the elbow. "Wait," he said. "There's more."

"I have to get back to work, Tío. I only have half an hour for lunch."

He looked at me in surprise, as if work was a word foreign to his vocabulary. "Down at the bank," I explained. "New Mexico State and Trust."

It still didn't register. I didn't have the heart, or the will, to remind him that he used to come up to my window once a week with La Tiendita's receipts. This was how I knew how much in arrears they were, what with customers' checks that bounced and a few of their own to food distributors that couldn't be paid because of insufficient funds.

"I have to go, Tío. See you later."

In his sad little voice he pleaded, "OK, Rafa, but come back and see me before it's too late." His wave was a feeble, priestly gesture of blessing to help me ward off the evil spirits in that den of iniquity where I worked. Jesus! I grabbed a pack of breath mints and tossed a coin on the counter as I hurried off.

That Sunday, as usual, I went over to Mamá's for pozole and sopaipillas. She outdid herself because she had asked me to bring a "nice" girl, one of my latest girls, to visit, and she wanted to make an impression. To let whomever know that I came from a nice family.

I brought Clara who I knew was the type Mamá wanted to see. Pop gave her one glance and then reburied his head in the Sunday paper. Meanwhile, Linda, who I really wanted to be with, was probably sleeping off the crazy party we went to the night before.

Mamá was all smiles the whole time, so I didn't dare bring up Tío Willie while Clara was around. Mamá even mouthed silent words of approval across the table to me when Clara wasn't looking. "Not like those tarts you see around town," I could almost hear Mamá say, "but nice." Tarts were young women in tight dresses who weren't absolutely flat chested, or those whose lipstick was too red. Nice meant they were polite to prospective mothers-in-law—"Sí, Señora. No, Señora."—went to early Mass instead of drunkard's Mass on Sundays, and smiled all the time even when they were miserable.

But I couldn't help thinking about Tío Willie. While I was avoiding Mamá's smiling face that beamed the message, "This may be the one," a childhood memory came back.

It must have been Christmas or New Year's or somebody's birthday. The whole family was at the house; it seemed like half of Los Rafas was parading in and out. The eating and drinking and laughing were going on in the front. I was hiding from my cousin Celia who was "it" in hide-and-seek, and I crept to the back room which was miraculously quiet. As I was about to tiptoe in, I heard a scuffle. Then some whispered angry words and a loud smack. Something told me not to go in, so I tiptoed quietly away. After awhile white-faced Mamá came into the crowd with a look that made Papá turn and pour himself another drink. Then, on the other side of the room, I saw Tío Willie rubbing the side of his face that was blood red.

We finished dinner and Mamá and Clara cleared the table. Then Mamá gave Papá a look, and he put down his paper and invited Clara outside to see his plum trees. I don't know which one of them looked more bored, Papá with his scowl or Clara with her perpetual smile.

I knew what was up, so before Mamá could say a word, I leaped in. "Tío Willie has heard La Llorona," I said. "He looks awful."

Mamá's face froze with a scowl set in concrete. "More likely the Virgin Mary crying because another sinner's getting ready to go to hell."

My mouth dropped open. Those were strong words from Mamá. I could often tell that she thought them, but I almost never heard her say them.

"He's fasting and praying for forty days and nights before he gets lifted up to heaven," I said. I smiled because I was sure Mamá saw what nonsense that was.

But the concrete face had hardened for good. "Ya dio las carnitas al diablo. Ahora quiere dar los huesitos a Dios."

What she meant was: He's already squandered his flesh on the devil; now he wants to bribe his way into heaven with the carcass. But it was just like down at the bank—insufficient funds.

Suddenly I had a weird vision. In my imagination I saw that las carnitas was offered by a butcher who looked just like Porky

Pig in the cartoons only with slick, black hair—probably a toupee—parted in the middle and combed to the sides. He twirled
his long mustachio with one hand and with the other patted his
blood-stained apron that strained over his ample gut. He stood
behind the counter at La Tiendita leering as the customers
came in.

I saw too that los huesitos were gathered by someone who
looked like old Sandoval, the barrio ragpicker of my childhood.
He clucked his tongue at his old horse who barely had the
strength to pull the wagon full of trash. Skinny, lugubrious Sandoval with the sad, pitiful face searching through the trash cans
for treasure. His long face getting sadder and sadder when all he
found was garbage. Even his old bag-of-bones of a horse was but
a few steps from the glue factory. Or maybe they boil bones for
gelatin, which is why I never eat Mamá's jello salad.

I shook my head back to reality and focused on Mamá. This
talk about Tío Willie had put her off so much she forgot to give
me the business about Clara. This was a nice one, she normally
would have said. When was I going to get married? Here I was
twenty-six years old already and living away from home in God
knows what kind of place. When was she going to see some
grandchildren?

I had heard it all before—too many times. So, knowing that
good things don't last forever, I grabbed Clara by the arm the
minute she and Papá came in and headed for the car.

"Come back again, honey," Mamá said, waving at Clara. Jesus!

The needle on the gas gauge was bouncing up and down off
empty, but I risked it and took Clara home first. She lived in Old
Town with her mother who must have been cut from the same
cookie mold as Mamá. Although it was early Sunday evening, I
could imagine the harangue at coming home an hour late with
that old excuse about running out of gas. Besides, as far as I was
concerned, the sooner I dumped Clara the better. I didn't want
her to get any ideas.

I made it to La Tiendita on air and imagination. The engine
died just in front of the pump. I got out to fill her up myself
since Tía was inside with a customer. As I unscrewed the gas cap
I heard this horrible singing coming from down near the river.

"O salutaris Hostia,
Quae caeli pandis o—o—stium:
Bella premunt hostilia,
Da robur, fer—"
Oh Christ, I thought. Now he's completely flipped. I walked
to the edge of the building and down the slope through the
cottonwoods. There he was in his pajamas and slippers, holding
a small wooden crucifix out at arm's length, facing the Río
Grande.

I stopped for a moment to let him finish his singing. He
didn't know all the words so I knew it couldn't last long unless he
decided to follow it with "Tangum Ergo" or a few Christmas
carols.

When he paused for a moment, having forgotten both tune
and words, I went up to him. If I hadn't moved quickly, he might
have started praying a rosary there on the bank of the river, and
I knew that would last forever.

"Tío?"

"Can you hear her?" he asked. "Shhh." We both listened, but
all I could hear was the lapping of the water. "You hear?" he
asked again. "She says they're making a place for me in heaven.
At the right hand of the Father, two steps below Jesus and right
alongside Saint Anthony."

"You better come in, Tío. You'll catch your death of cold out
here."

He kissed the crucifix and came along docilely. The door to
the house was locked so I took him through the store. Tía and
her customer saw me leading this wild man in pajamas past the
bread shelves through the door into the adjoining little house,
but they went on with their business as if it was an everyday
occurrence.

The cash register clunked, then the bell jingled and the door
slammed, and I heard Tía Annie approaching. She had popped
into the room when Tío, who sat on the edge of the bed, said, "I
saw the Virgin Mary today."

Her shout startled me. "You're crazy!" Her face was contorted in anger. "I was changing the sheets on that filthy bed of
yours, and you saw me with one of them spread out."

I envisioned it clearly. Tía flapping the sheet out to spread it on the bed. Tío looking from the bathroom or wherever for just that split second when it looked like a shroud draped over this female figure.

Tío's eyes widened in fright, and he turned away and slipped under the blankets facing the wall.

"You know what else?" Tía Annie said. "Tell him what else," she challenged Tío, but she didn't wait for an answer. "I had to sweep a hundred empty corn chip bags and God knows how many melon rinds from under the bed. That's his forty days and forty nights fasting. ¡Mentiras!"

I took pity on the groan from the bed and ushered Tía back out to the store. But she was pretty worked up, and there was no way that I could stop her from talking at me.

"He's a wreck," she said. "He's dying." For a moment she looked like she was going to cry. "Ruined liver from drinking too much," she went on. "Ruined lungs from smoking too much—he can hardly breathe. Ruined other things from too much the devil-only-knows what else." Then the tears started.

"It'll be all right, auntie."

She shook her head vigorously in disagreement and wiped at her eyes with the back of her hand, leaving a grease streak from having checked under the hood of some paisano's car. "He used to charm the crows out of the cornfields when he played his guitar and sang. A voice sweet as honey. Always with a joke. Always the life of the party. Everybody loved him." Then she gave me a piercing look as if she were reading something written on my face.

"Your mother worries about you, Sonny." Oh, God, I thought. Here it comes again. "She says you're running around with Linda Padilla." I blinked in surprise. How had Mamá learned about Linda? "You know those Padillas," Tía said. "Hot blooded. That was your uncle's downfall."

I didn't bother to ask whether she meant his hot blood or Padilla women. I remembered the broken hand—"Caught in the door," Mamá explained—that someone later told me was from an irate husband catching Tío Willie with the wrong wife; the husband said that never again would Willie strum a guitar or pinch a behind. I remembered the broken nose—"Ran into a door"—again the door was the fist of a man angry over the

wrong woman. And I looked at the poor, falsely-accused door
and remembered that I had better things to do. I didn't need a
lecture from Mamá second-hand through Tía Annie.

Tía followed me, yammering away as I put two dollars worth
of gas in the car, but I tuned her out. Then she refused to take
my money, and that made me mad. It was bad enough putting
up with Tío Willie, but to flaunt poverty was compounding
madness by stupidity.

She was still talking when I thrust the crumpled bills into the
pocket of her sweater and roared off. She might have stayed
there another hour for all I know. As far as I was concerned, I
saw little difference between that and Tío Willie singing on the
bank of the river.

Luckily for my morale, Papá dropped into the bank the next
day, and we went to Woolworth's on my coffee break. "Sonny, I
hope you don't mind my saying so, but your mother was really
taken with Clara." He paused the way he always does to check my
reaction. "But to tell the truth—" He put on his sour face and
shook his head slowly. I knew what he meant. He thought she
was a loser.

"Don't worry," I said. "Clara is just a friend." There was an
audible sigh of relief.

"But there is one thing that bothers me," I went on. "Both
Mamá and Tía Annie seem to think I'm going to hell in a hand-
basket. They keep warning me I'll end up like Tío Willie."

"Those women." Again he shook his head. "Let me tell you
something. Years ago when your mother and I were first married, we went to Juárez on vacation, and she kept pointing out
these women to me. 'There,' she'd say. 'That one on the street
corner in the red dress. That's a prostitute. There. That one
smiling in front of the café. That's another.'

"It shocked me. Most of all that your sweet innocent mother,
a little girl from the country, would know what a whore looked
like. But also that at least half the women on the streets of Juárez
must be streetwalkers. I have to confess that I stared. I didn't
know what a whore looked like. They looked just like any other
women to me.

"When I got to know your mother better, I realized that
that's the way she was. I shouldn't tell you this—but—oh, hell.

You're a grown man. Anyway. After our honeymoon she made me move the crucifix from over the head of the bed to the living room. 'It's not right,' she said, 'to have Him watching.'

"So you see, Sonny. These are funny women. They think all men are just—Well. Animals I guess."

"You know that's not true, Papá."

He nodded, but I didn't know if it was for me or for the waitress to pour him another cup of coffee. "I'll never understand women," he said. "Even your mother. Maybe that's part of what makes them so interesting.

"But one thing. Don't go taking your mother or your aunt too seriously. There are very few men like Willie, pobre. Most of us have more sense. And as for you, someday you'll meet the one. But whoever and whenever, it had better be *your* choice. Just yours. Because you're going to have to put up with her the rest of your life."

I appreciated that. Almost as much as I appreciated that he hadn't asked me about Linda Padilla. I'm sure he was dying to recommend to me a "nice" Spanish girl who was docile and obedient, but he respected me enough to keep it to himself.

A few nights later I was cleaning the mess in my apartment when Cousin Charlie brought me the sad news. His father had gone to sleep the night before and never waked up. Tía Annie had phoned him right away, and when he and his wife got there, auntie was sitting on her old rocking chair beside the bed.

"Well," she greeted them. "Look for yourself. His body has not ascended into heaven, but then why should it? He never kept a promise to me in his whole life." Then she started to cry and didn't stop until the doctor came and knocked her out with a sedative.

After that there was the old-fashioned velorio and the rosary in San Felipe Church in Old Town and the whole bit.

The day of the funeral a fleet of Cadillac limousines brought us from Ortega's Funeral Home to the cemetary. On the way to where they were breaking new ground we passed the old section. I could see the generations of Rafas there, including Grandpa and Grandma. Then my mother's family, the Archuletas.

Everyone piled out of the limousines and their beat-up old cars and pickup trucks and gathered near the open grave. I kept hoping Tío Willie had an insurance policy, becaue if he hadn't, Tía Annie was going to have to sell the tienda to pay for this parade.

The thing that really got me though, was there was a head-stone standing on display where everybody had to see it as they faced the grave. "Guillermo Durán," it read. "Beloved husband of Anne Archuleta Durán. Faithful through eternity." Jesus! She must have ordered it a month before he died. Sort of her hope chest for the hereafter.

The people gathered, and the priest said his holy words and sprinkled water all around. When it broke up, Tía Annie was leaning on Mamá and crying.

"I don't know if I can stand it alone," Tía said between sobs. "Forty years is a long time."

"You have your family," Mamá said. But it's not the same, I thought. Then Mamá looked around startled for her purse, and I left the side of the limousine and ran back.

My nerves must have been jumpy, because as I bent to the ground to pick up the purse, I swear I heard something roll over the grave. It sounded like old Sandoval's wagon come to pick up the bones. I felt clammy and a little faint as I looked up and saw both their faces: the carnicero who looked like Porky Pig and old Sandoval, both on the wooden seat of the wagon beckoning to-ward me. Then the wagon disappeared gradually into the ground, and I knew heaven was not their destination.

When I got back to the limousine Papá gave me a funny look. "Are you all right?" he asked. "You look like you've seen a ghost."

I shuddered as I handed Mamá her purse. The two women hugged each other and cried, a real pair of lloronas. Then I swear I heard the squeaky wagon wheels give one more turn and fade into the earth.

What could I do after that? It was inevitable. Two months later Linda and I announced our engagement.

Be-Bop Rock

Not many women are lucky enough to be married to someone like Emiliano Zapata Rosca. My Pata. He's a teacher, a very honorable profession, and makes a good enough living that I don't have to work unless I want to. Not like some poor women, of whom I could name a few but won't, who either share the burden or carry the whole load for their so-called men.

And unlike men in the old country, Pata is ever faithful. There, the minute a Mexican man gains a little success in life, he takes a young blond mistress while "Mamá" is left at home to tend children and be taken out on Sundays to church and a family outing for public display. Well, you know what I think about that!

But like I said, not everyone is lucky. Especially Carmelita, the next oldest of my three sisters (I'm the youngest). The latest of her once-in-awhile letters came yesterday.

"Dear Lola,

I don't suppose you heard the tragic news yet. They found Be-Bop under one of those green benches in that park in downtown L.A. where all the crazies go to rant and rave on soapboxes. Just at the bottom of Wino Hill. There was a brown paper bag cradled in his left arm; the bottle inside was empty. The police said it wasn't booze though, but mostly a drug overdose with a little muscatel on the side. When they went to his room in one of those fleabag wino hotels, all they found was a picture of our son, Jimmy, and that clipping from the newspaper when Jimmy almost went on the stage. That and Be-Bop's guitar case, which was empty except for some dirty socks. I guess he pawned the guitar."

I would have called her right then, but I didn't have her telephone number. The return address on the envelope was a new one. From the tone of her letter she seemed to take it pretty well except when she wrote about Jimmy losing his daddy. The poor little darling had never stopped asking when daddy was coming home even though it had been almost a year.

When I got to that part of the letter I had to go outside and make sure that Lolita and Junior were all right. I stood on the lawn for awhile until Lolita shouted at me from the neighbor's yard, "What's the matter, Mama?" I shook my head and went back into the house, blinking my eyes and remembering what must have been the beginning of the end a little over a year ago.

They were still living together in San Diego then. Carmelita had been married to Be-Bop Espinosa, whose real first name was Armando, for about four years. It had been a stormy marriage, not least because our parents had so violently opposed the match.

Carmelita had always been the rebellious sister and at no time more so than when she married this crazy musician. Papá had flatly declared that he would not attend the wedding. But then Mamá had worked on him, telling him he ought to be thankful they were getting married at all instead of just living together in sin like so many do these days. Like Mamá always said: If it ain't legal, it's nothing. At the last minute Papá relented and gave the bride away, but he disappeared from church right after the ceremony.

After that I became the family liaison; no one else could tolerate Be-Bop for more than two minutes at a time. And San Diego is only a couple of hours by freeway from where we live near Southwestern U. Pata had to prepare for a conference in San Francisco that autumn so I went alone one weekend while he stayed home to work and babysit.

I could tell that things were not going well although Carmelita put up a cheerful front. The smile stayed frozen on her lips too long, and if you watched her eyes you could tell how she really felt. "Everything's great!" she'd say animatedly. "Just great!" And she'd bob her head up and down for emphasis. But her startled eyes mirrored something other than great.

Their little miracle child as our oldest sister unkindly referred to him—he had been born six months after the wedding—was three and a half years old then. About the age of our

Junior and a year older than Lolita. Jimmy was an absolute darling, not like his father at all.

Be-Bop's band had a gig that Saturday night at some club over in National City so Carmelita and I had the afternoon and evening to ourselves. "Everything's great! Just great!" she repeated for the dozenth time. I kept wondering when she was going to let up and really level with me. But it was all girlish recollections and gossip about the people we knew in high school and in the old neighborhood in San Diego. Lots of giggles, but behind the laughter her unspoken sorrow.

"Be-Bop has a new guitar," she said. "It used to belong to Carlos Santana. I told him it it was a good thing he hadn't bought one from one of those rock stars who smash them on stage." She started to smile, but I read her mind, and she seemed to sense it and the smile faded: With Be-Bop's luck he would have paid top price for an unusable, splintered wreck, then bragged about it.

"And anyway," she said. Her voice lowered almost to a whisper, and for the first time I sensed a seriousness in what she was about to say. Her brittle eyes had turned soft and moist. "Anyway," she repeated, "I'm going to have another baby."

Her nonsequitur startled me; I blamed it on her troubled state. "Oh, Carmelita!" I squealed and gave her a hug and a kiss and drew back to inspect her. Her abdomen was slim and flat as ever.

"It won't be for months yet," she said. Then she dropped onto the tired sofa and burst into tears.

I didn't dare ask her if she didn't want it, so I said, "What's the matter, Carmelita?" Her answer was to cry even harder. I sat beside her and put my arms around her as she cried it out.

Finally she calmed down and looked at me as if remembering my question of minutes before. "Oh, Lola. What's Jimmy going to do when I tell him?"

"He'd love a little sister or brother," I said.

Carmelita looked over my shoulder past me, and I almost turned around to see if anyone was there. I knew there really wasn't. It was just her way of hopscotching from the subject. When she turned her gaze back to me, she was in control again and wiped her tear-streaked cheeks before she spoke.

"Be-Bop is doing very well," she said. I wanted to believe her in spite of what I'd heard from the rest of the family. "Some disc jockeys are coming to hear them at the club tonight. Be-Bop said one of them has connections with a record company in Hollywood. It may be their big break."

It's a quirk of human nature to believe what one must. In the struggle between insanity and belief in falsehoods, belief wins the early skirmishes and sometimes that is enough for a lifetime. I hoped so for Carmelita's sake. From what I heard, Be-Bop bounced from one band to another at the insistence of the bands, because of one outrageous thing or another. I'd heard he'd been with one group for six months, but that was the longest. They'd finally kicked him out for exposing himself on stage in the middle of a performance.

"What's the name of the group?" I asked.

She looked at me solemn faced with no trace of emotion. "Last Chance," she said. I shivered. "They're thinking of going into country western," she added softly, "but now they're a heavy metal rock group."

After Jimmy was put to bed we finished the last of the six-pack, sitting in the kitchen ignoring the sink full of dishes. Carmelita had that faraway look in her eye again, staring over my shoulder at the wall just below the plumber's advertising calendar that still showed last month.

"You've been married just about a year more than we have, haven't you?" she asked. I nodded. "How's Pata?"

"Fine."

"Do you remember when we were single? Way back then?" I nodded again. She flicked a bright-eyed gleam at me. "Remember that time we double-dated the Chavalo brothers? Before we knew that they always got into fights at the drive-in?"

I remembered. I had never been so frightened in my life. It wasn't just the Chavalos fighting those other boys. There was enough of that in our high school and our neighborhood, even if I didn't like it. It was the tough girls with those other two boys. While they were fighting, these two girls came up to us. One of them pulled a hairpin out of her pompador that was as long as a dagger and stared hatefully at me. That's when Carmelita and I jumped in the car and locked the doors and leaned on the horn until someone called the police.

"You were going with Jaime Osorio then," I said, "and you

dated the Chavalo brother with the low-rider to make Jaime
jealous. You made me double-date because you wanted a chaper-
one. God, those Chavalos were ugly—the whole family."

All of a sudden she burst into tears. I thought maybe it was
too much beer and memories of happier, crazy times; or maybe
she was thinking about that little baby growing inside her.

"Oh, Lola," she said after she had calmed down once more. "I
never told anyone before in my life. Never! Not even the priest
in confession." My hair was too drunk to stand on end, but it
tried. "Promise me," she said. "Promise me you won't dare repeat
this to a soul. On our mother's sacred honor." I promised.

"Jimmy—" she began. Then she started to cry again. When
she quieted down she said, "I owe Be-Bop a lot. More than you'll
ever know."

"Sure."

Then she was staring over my shoulder again at the plumber's calendar. "No," she finally said. "There's no sense burdening
you with my problems." But her look said that what she really
meant was that there were still things she wasn't willing to tell
me.

It quieted down after than. Carmelita made a half-hearted
offer to go to the liquor store for another six-pack while I stayed
with Jimmy, but I was already nodding, trying to stay awake.

We turned on the late movie instead and sat staring across the
room at this teeny tiny TV set that must have been two inches
across. Between its fuzzy picture and my blurry eyesight I drifted
off to sleep.

During a commercial I woke up with a start, the way you do
when you're travelling and you stay in a strange place. I looked
around trying to orient myself, my heart pounding, until I saw
Carmelita quietly sitting with a river of tears rolling down her
cheeks. Then I saw the TV screen again. The commercial was
over, and it was the same dumb Western we'd been watching. It
should have made her laugh, so I realized how bad things must
really be. I mumbled some excuse, went to the room I shared
with Jimmy who was asleep in the crib that he was outgrowing,
undressed in the dark, and slipped into the cold, narrow bed.

I thought it was a dream at first. The acrid smell almost like
cigarette smoke but not quite. Two thumps, one right after the

other. Finally the smell of wine before the male voice in my
dream tried to whisper but did not succeed; it came out loud like
a deaf person answering a question. "Hey, man. I didn't know
you had a surprise for me."

I woke, my eyes popping open in fright, as the edge of the
bed sagged under someone's weight. "Hey, Be-Bop, man. Let's
wake her up so we can party."

"Get out of here!" I said, more angry than frightened now
that I realized what it was.

The boozy breath leaned across the bed toward me. "Hey,
chickie, it's only me. Good old—"

I screamed. The drunk fell off the bed onto the floor. Jimmy
started to cry. The sounds of running feet grew louder then
stopped as the light clicked on.

"Get this—this pig—out of here!" I screamed.

Be-Bop was in the doorway weaving unsteadily, his eyes slits
of red, stoned out of his mind. Carmelita approached from
behind him, tying the belt of a wrap around her waist.

A sloppy grin crossed Be-Bop's face. "Hey, Lola." Then he
looked down at the floor and started to laugh. "Don't let him
scare you. That's only our drummer." The words came out pain-
fully slow, and he smiled all the while as if at some private joke
that I couldn't see.

"Get him out of here!" I yelled. "Before I call the police."

Be-Bop frowned and his bloodshot eyes narrowed so much I
thought they would squirt blood. He put out a hand, palm forward, like he was stopping traffic. "No fuzz, Lola. We don't even
allow that word in this house. Not unless it's a curse."

A look passed among the three of them, while Jimmy whim-
pered, ignored by all. Then Be-Bop started to laugh at the
drummer who was crawling on the floor looking for his shoes.
Carmelita finally went over to the crib and picked up Jimmy who
had started to climb out.

"I'm sorry," she said to me. Then to the others. "Everybody
out! Don't you dare bother Lola again!"

The light went out, and the door closed behind them. Now I
was in total darkness, wide awake, the sound of angry voices
assaulting me through the paper-thin walls.

I tried not to hear. I don't want to listen to other people's personal quarrels. Especially people I love. But it was impossible. You can always shut your eyes tight until you can't see, but there's no way you can completely close your ears.

It came to me in a kaleidoscope of anger, accusations, rebuttals. Someone came threatening from the loan company this morning; he'd be back Monday. It's too bad that the drummer's girl friend kicked him out, but there was no room for him here. Especially not at four o'clock in the morning. And do your goddamn partying somewhere else.

When it wasn't women—¡putas! Carmelita shouted at one point—it was money. Where was the money from this gig? Where was the fifty dollars he promised? The rent was overdue.

Oh, Jesus. I wanted to go out there and punch him out myself. I finally put my hands on my ears, hoping it would block out the horrible squabble, but one more scream from Carmelita pierced through.

"No!" she shouted. "Not Jimmy!"

"It's our fortune," Be-Bop said. "You talk about money—that's where it's at."

"No!"

Then I heard the slap of flesh on flesh. I pulled the covers over my head and prayed to God for forgiveness for the anger and hate that I felt. By the time I calmed down to where I could drift back to sleep, daylight was gradually brightening the room, and I thought: What the hell. It's too late now. I might as well get up.

Jimmy was sleeping peacefully, his tiny bare feet sticking through the slats of the crib. I pulled the blanket down around his feet, then dressed quietly. When I peeked into the front room, I saw a body sprawled across the floor, uncovered, a rasping drunken snore coming from it like the rise and fall of ocean waves beating against the silence. I didn't recognize him so it must have been the drummer. The animal!

When I looked up, my eyes met Carmelita's. She was wrapped in a blanket sitting stiffly on a chair. Silently I mouthed the words: "I'm going to Mass." But when her puzzled frown showed that she didn't understand, I made a sign of the cross and motioned my head toward the front door. She nodded and quietly rose to wash and dress.

We walked in silence through the cool morning, hand in hand like when we were little girls and Papá would give us each a nickel for the collection plate and a penny for ourselves for afterwards. All through Mass I tried not to look at Carmelita because I knew I would remember old times. We had made our First Communions together even though she is a year older than me. She came down with the mumps the year she was supposed to and had to wait another year. The two of us had shared our beautiful white dresses and our sense of sin and confession, worrying about whether the wafer would stick to the roofs of our mouths and turn into the blood of Christ because we were bad and couldn't swallow it.

After Mass we sat quietly while the old ladies who were the ones who attended early Mass emptied the church. We were the last to leave. Afterwards we stood out by the bus stop in the morning sun and watched the streets slowly crawl to life.

"I think I'd better leave, Carmelita," I said.

She put her trembling little hands tentatively on my arm as if trying to decide whether or not to hold me back. "I'm sorry, Lola."

"I'm just in the way," I said, "and if I stay I'm liable to say something I'll be sorry for."

Her grip tightened on the sleeve of my coat. "Stay today. Be-Bop wants you to be there to see Jimmy." When I hesitated, she said, "Please."

"All right."

After awhile we came to a little café down the boulevard that was open and went in for coffee. It was still early, but there were a few solitary men at the counter leaning over their cups like they were trying to forget last night if only their headaches would let them. An older woman and a little girl who must have been her granddaughter were at a table chatting sleepily over hot chocolate.

"I want to move out of here," Carmelita said. "As soon as Be-Bop gets his big break. The schools are terrible, and there are nothing but gangs and drunks."

"Sure," I said.

"Be-Bop's not so bad," she said. "At least he always comes back home." When I looked at her she was staring at the half-full cup of coffee, and I could see that she really didn't believe what she said. There was a tightness to her face so that the bones shone through like a skeleton.

"You could always move back in with the folks," I said.

Her eyes snapped. "No way."

We finished our coffee in silence and walked back to their place where a red-eyed Be-Bop was bustling about. "We've got to be at El Serape by eleven o'clock, and I can't find any clean clothes for Jimmy."

By the time everything was all ready, Carmelita was a nervous wreck, and I found myself clenching a fist and praying that Be-Bop would stay out of reach so something wouldn't happen. Then we hopped into his pickup truck, Jimmy on Carmelita's lap with a bag of props on the floor under her knees. Before we got more than a few blocks, Be-Bop touched me for a two-dollar "loan" for enough gas to get us there and back.

"You're going to love it," he said. "You'll see. It's amateur afternoon, but I'm not going to tell you more than that. It'll spoil the surprise."

There's nothing as sad as a night club when the neon lights are off and daylight shows it in all its dismal tawdriness. The place still reeked of stale beer and sweat, even though it had had since two AM to air out. The paint was peeling and the help looked like B-girls or race track touts.

Be-Bop strutted through waving hands at everybody, reveling in their attention. "Hey," one shouted, "is that the little champ?" Be-Bop beamed a toothy grin and nodded.

He left us at a table, then took Jimmy to the bar where he ordered a hair of the dog and stood the little darling up on a barstool while people crowded around him.

"He shouldn't have done that," Carmelita said peevishly. "Jimmy will get scared." All the way over I sensed her nerves getting tighter and tighter, and now she appeared to be in a perfect funk. She looked angrily across the room toward the bar. "Oh, I just hate it!" she said. "I hate everything about it. Is this any kind of life for Jimmy?" She snapped her head at me and glared.

One of the waiters brought over two drinks and set them down on our table. Be-Bop grinned at us, pointed to the glasses, and gave us a crisp salute as if to say "You're welcome" to the thanks neither of us offered. Carmelita stared sullenly at the table top, and I watched the crowd. Family mostly, and friends, come to see their favorite amateur take that first step on the stairway to the stars.

After awhile there was a stirring on the stage—the bandstand really—which was a platform raised about a foot or so above the dance floor. Be-Bop took Jimmy by the hand and walked him over to a chair where he sat him down alongside their bag of props.

"This is it," Carmelita said, with a kind of finality that made me think she wasn't talking about the upcoming performance but about something else more basic and more important.

The combo blared a lively tune, and the MC hopped up to the microphone. "Ladies and gentlemen—" It had started.

The contestants were all ages although Jimmy was the youngest by far. Two girls in their early teens did a Spanish dance in costume, one dressed as a torero and the other as a señorita. A large, Indian-dark, heavily powdered woman sang a Mexican ranchero with lots of wailing and vocal throbbing. An intense young man sang a love song in limpid Spanish. Then Be-Bop leaned over and whispered in Jimmy's ear as the MC hopped back onto the stage.

"¡Damas y caballeros! Ladies and gentlemen! Let's give a big welcome to our next contestant, the world's youngest impressionist, Jimmy Espinosa!"

Jimmy walked on stage followed by Be-Bop carrying the bag, while the MC adjusted the microphone down to Jimmy's height. Be-Bop squatted down beside him and reached into the bag of props; Jimmy peered over to see what was coming first.

On came the high top hat and out came a fake cigar and after Be-Bop whispered the first cue, "W.C. Fields," Jimmy mimicked in a nasal whine, "Yes—s, yes—s, Ye—s indeed." It was enough. Everybody howled.

The top hat came off and two fake black eyebrows went on his forehead and a black, square mustache onto his upper lip. Jimmy flicked an imaginary ash off the end of the cigar which he held out at arm's length. "Groucho Marx," came the cue. After a few rolls of the eyebrows came the words, "Say the secret woid and you win one hundred dollahs." The burst of laughter was even louder this time.

Then, of course, out came the cowboy hat. No cue was necessary as Jimmy hitched his thumbs into his belt, shifted his weight slowly from left leg to right, and drawled out in Spanish, "All right, pilgrim. One false move, and you're a dead man." John Wayne! In Spanish no less. They loved it.

I looked over at Carmelita. Her face was grim and full of anger. "Listen to them," she hissed. "They're laughing and that poor child doesn't even know why. This is it!" she said. "I'm going to leave Be-Bop, and I'm going to tell him the truth."

All I could do was look at her. The laughter broke into loud applause, and her face turned deep red with anger. "Look at him. Just look at him." She meant Be-Bop who was bowing as deeply as Jimmy at the end of the act.

The room became restlessly inattentive at the next act. The off-key soprano's terrified eyes showed that she knew that the audience had gotten away from her and wasn't coming back.

"I can't live like this anymore," Carmelita said. "I told him this was the last straw. I don't want him using Jimmy to make up for his own lack of success." She sat silent for a moment, tapping the table with a forefinger. She seemed to be puzzling something over. For the first time the anger dissipated, and she seemed near to tears.

"Oh, Lola. I've made such a mess of my life. Why do I believe these men?" She stared at the stage, not seeing the soprano who was hurrying off as if fleeing for her life. "I owe Be-Bop a lot." Then she turned and looked at me intently, and I knew she was going to share a confidence. "No one else in the world knows," she said, "not even Be-Bop. But Jimmy isn't his."

My mouth fell open. I looked at the side of the stage and saw father and—no. I couldn't say that now— I saw the two of them beaming in triumph. For the first time I looked hard at Jimmy as if blinders had been removed from my eyes. My heart was pounding, and I was totally confused like I had been sleep walking and a shock woke me in the middle of an intersection with cars zooming by me in every direction.

But I saw it. From clear across the room I saw it. The curly hair. The eyes almost green but sometimes looking brown. The

face that would be unbearably handsome in another ten or fifteen years and was baby-adorable now. I saw Jaime Osorio as a
child.

I looked at Carmelita in shock, and she nodded. "Be-Bop
thinks he's his," she said. Then she started to laugh, and I got
angry and wanted to slap her. "Jaime wouldn't marry me," she
said. "Be-Bop was crazy about me. Oh, God. Don't tell the folks.
It would kill them."

Who needed to tell them? If they ever took one look at this
grandson of theirs they'd know. While up near the stage Be-Bop
was still beaming like a proud father.

I was numb the rest of the afternoon. When they announced
the winner and presented twenty-five dollars in cash to little
Jimmy who immediately handed it to Be-Bop. As we drove back
in the pickup with Be-Bop chattering like a monkey about how
Jimmy was going to be the new male child TV star.

Still numb, I packed my bag and got ready to say goodbye.
Meanwhile Carmelita seemed to have calmed down. Her mind
was made up. After I'd gone I was sure they would have it out.

"Later, Lola baby," Be-Bop said. "The next time you see us
our names will be in lights." He spread his hand and moved it
grandly across the front of his face. "Be-Bop Espinosa and Son,
entertainers extraordinaire." The look on Carmelita's face said
something different, and I was almost sorry for the shock that
Be-Bop would be getting soon.

They were still waving when I pulled away from the curb and
looked up at the rear view mirror. As I drove I began to think:
Oh, God. Whatever happened to soft-stringed guitars and sere-
nades under señoritas' balconies? Whatever happened to gallant
suitors and the bliss of the first time on your wedding night? Oh,
God, whatever happened to love?

That was the last time I saw Carmelita. Somehow I was always too busy when the thought of another visit crossed my
mind. There were times when I began to wonder what cruel god
had made her so different from the rest of the family. And if she
had really told Be-Bop the truth about Jimmy, though Be-Bop
would have ended up the way he did no matter what.

I picked up the letter and read the last part of it once more.
"Lola, I sometimes wish I was on better terms with the folks so

that Jimmy could see his grandparents. But then I'm afraid for them to see him. You know why.

"Anyway, there's this guy I met down at the café where I work. He's real nice and loves kids and—"

I couldn't read any more. What was the use? We are what we are, and sometimes if we're lucky we learn a little on our way through life. I picked up the envelope and looked at the address and thought reluctantly that it was about time for a trip to San Diego. I guess somebody has to try to keep the family together, though God knows, sometimes I wonder why.

Grace in Unexpected Places

God did not appear to Ricardo Peña as an invisible voice of thunder. It was more as if He winked. And when God winks, the universe winks, which is an awesome jolt for a mere mortal. Especially for an enlightened skeptic of this secular age.

True, Ricardo lamented the old institutions of belief that seemed to have lost their way. Many had grown to a certain critical mass (a "scientific" term although he was no scientist) beyond which institutions take on a life of their own and exist for their own sakes. It was with such an attitude that he entered college some years ago and took his leave of the Holy Roman Catholic Church, way of truth, shepherd of lost lambs, refuge of his forbears.

Yet, for all his supposed independence from the mystical and mysterious, he felt a void like a subtle, uncomfortable itch that had to be scratched, especially when later his wife Sharon and he had a son of their own. It led them to join that legion of seekers rummaging through the cults and sects of the time like bargain hunters wondering what the catch was because so many promised so much for so little. Until he realized that their so little was the same old price: unquestioning devotion and complete surrender.

Their current guru, whom Ricardo followed hesitantly, led a movement of the well educated, professionally employed, and affluent. The initial appeal was decidedly altruistic. (Do you want to save the world?) Later it was flavored with a hint of guilt. (You are lucky. You are affluent. Why aren't you saving the world?) It was rationalized with the psychological heavily influenced by Maslow; they were already sufficiently blessed with Maslow's trinity: things physical, mental, and emotional, and were ready to move on to a greater goal.

In spite of the appeals, only a vague feeling hooked its barbs into the void Ricardo felt. It was the vestige of his Catholic youth, the memory of original sin whispering its uneasy guilt.

"Ricardo!" his wife nagged early one evening. "It's next Saturday. Are you going?"

Exasperation responded to annoyance. "Tonight there's a group meeting. Thursday night a leadership class. And Friday night we substitute as assistant leaders for a beginners' group."

"Are you going?"

He heard the low murmur of the television set from the family room where ten-year Scott was sprawled on the carpet watching. In his imagination Ricardo heard their group leader chiding him once again for his "resistance." Although no one ever said it, in this group "resistance" was "bad."

"Ricardo! Are you going?"

"No. I'm taking Scotty to the football game."

He waited for the clouds to part and the thunderous voice from heaven to upbraid him. What happened instead was that Sharon's face grew longer and longer, a dolorous El Greco of accusation.

"You're not giving it a chance."

"I'm giving it too much of a chance. Tonight, Thursday, Friday."

"Then I won't go!" She said it in such a way that it meant: And it'll be your fault.

"God is everywhere," he said. "Even in football stadiums."

"That isn't funny."

But when he told Scotty, the boy shouted hurray. And late Saturday morning they filled their thermos with cocoa, their pockets with packets of shortbread cookies, and bicycled to the game.

The home team was called the Indians—it was a time when such nicknames did not embarrass, before the ethnically sensitive protested and the ethnically assaulted capitulated. The visiting team from the great northwest was quarterbacked by a real Indian whose name was Sonny Sixkiller. It was also at a point in Ricardo's life when he was not ashamed to acknowledge the Indian part of his ancestry. The game, in a sense, was like coming home.

Sonny Sixkiller dashed skillfully back and forth, his right

arm a powerful bow slinging arrows to his receivers. The home team, Indians in name only, lumbered after him, too slow, too late, too clumsy. Scotty saw some schoolmates and joined them on the stadium walkway. He paced anxiously on the fringe, trying to break into the not too responsive group. He was still there, edging his way in among them when the third quarter got under way.

From high in the north end of the stadium Ricardo watched Sonny Sixkiller dance his war dance, befuddling the charging Indians. Midway through the quarter, he looked toward the open end of the stadium into a grove of tall trees. At first he thought that his eyes were playing tricks. The grove seemed to fade and waver, like a mirage floating on particles of heated desert air. Then the trees snapped into focus, clean and sharp, as if viewed through an old-fashioned stereopticon. They stood out with a dimensional intensity unlike anything he had ever seen. He could see into, through, and around them all at once.

At the same instant, he was overwhelmed with a sense of awe. Not only could he not believe his eyes, but the top of his skull felt like it had unhinged and was flooded with light. A play must have gotten underway, because he could hear the roar of the crowd. He knew that if he continued to stare at the trees he would faint in the midst of sixty thousand screaming maniacs.

Along with this fear and awe, there was an incredible feeling that he himself had faded, had melted into the trees and the stadium, into the crowd and Sonny Sixkiller. He too wavered like the verdant grove. Some great hand on the universal switch flicked it on and off, pulsing this powerful emotion through him. He was overwhelmed by a sense of oneness with everything in the universe like nothing he had ever felt before. He waited to hear the thunder from the clouds, but there were no clouds and no thunder.

Time disappeared. Ricardo could not remember where. Suddenly it was the fourth quarter. He had tried to sneak other peeks at the grove of trees, but each time the powerful feeling would engulf him, and he looked away in panic. Scotty must have come back because Ricardo heard his voice in the distance.

"Dad, are you all right?"

He answered from far off, "Yes."

"You look funny, dad. Sort of greenish."

Ricardo tried to smile, fumbling to pat his son on the shoulder. Then, in his mind, he heard not the voice of thunder, but a small whisper that he recognized as himself, speaking in the accent of a Jewish peddler.

"Cut out the middle man," it said. "I can get it for you wholesale."

If it had not been such a serious matter, he might have smiled. Instead he looked across the stadium to the grove of trees. Again they faded, then snapped sharply into focus, though without the intensity of that first time.

"See," the small whisper said. "Go directly to the source. Deal with the Chairman of the Board."

Ricardo watched for awhile this time, less fearful, not overpowered by the sense that he would be struck down. "Hello," he said in his mind. The grove of trees pulsed at him, then faded.

When the game ended, a defeat for the home team, they waited for the disgruntled crowd to clear, then walked to the exit.

"You look better now, Dad." Scotty's voice had lost its anxiety.

As they bicycled through traffic, Ricardo glanced at the clusters of trees along the way: giant oaks, sycamores, redwoods. Each time the sight warmed him, and he knew that if he stopped and stared at them long enough, he would see God.

As they neared home, it suddenly struck him that his searching days were over. He needed no guru; one would only be in the way. All he had to do was turn to the world around him, to the omnipresence, and know that everything was as it should be.

The house was empty when they entered. Sharon had gone to the workshop alone. It was now clear that when she got back, Ricardo would have to tell her that his guru days were over.

"Thanks, Dad," Scotty said. "It was a neat game. Too bad we lost."

Ricardo smiled.

Philomena

My youngest son, Junior, had taken the telephone message like a typical ten-year old. When Gabriel and I had finally come home from the police station, I picked up the note from where it was anchored by the corner of the phone and read the garbled message on the torn, unprinted edge of the afternoon newspaper that my husband had yet to read.

"Grandma Philomena. Homecoming. Grandpa." The pencil-scrawled words were all but unreadable.

I crumbled the scrap of note and threw it on the floor, bursting into tears. This is all I need, I thought. Just what I should have expected. It never rains but it pours.

Gabe was not there to comfort me. He had marched our fourteen-year old son, Michael, the reason for our visit to the police station, straight through the living room to the back bedroom and slammed the door.

Junior had disappeared, leaving the house unlocked. God knows what was missing. I didn't have the strength to lift my head and look across the room to see if the TV set was still there. Even if I had, I probably couldn't have seen through the waterfall of tears.

My mother, Philomena, has said often enough that she was a saint, while I, her oldest child Rose, was the one in the family who was "different." Even as a child I knew Mamá meant "black sheep." Even now that I'm almost forty years old, it still bothers me to be the outcast and the one least loved by Mamá. Every daughter has a mother, although every mother doesn't have a daughter. Maybe that doesn't make much sense, but to me it's a reason for wanting to be more than "different."

Philomena had been the name of a saint and martyr, Mamá had told me often enough over the years—daily it seemed like during my childhood. She always tried to live up to that name, she'd add. Let that be a lesson to you, Rose.

Only Rose was the name of a saint, too. Rosa de Lima, the first New World saint. Although I must say she was a sick one who rubbed pepper on her beautiful face to ruin her complexion and took a garland of flowers from her mother and fastened it by sticking a large pin into her head. Crazy. Just crazy. Mamá named me after the wrong saint. It was she who should have been named Rose, although she reveled in Philomena, probably because not much is known about her and she could attach to it any meaning she wanted.

The first howl from the back bedroom shattered my tearful silence. I held my breath in surprise, then heard the whop of the belt and second howl. I started crying again, only this time for Michael.

Is this the way to do it? I thought. Gabe and I had quarreled about it often enough, but I still wasn't convinced. Then the solemn, freckled face of the juvenile officer loomed out of the air, and I could hear him again.

"Mr. and Mrs. Padilla, do you really have your son under control? I know what the scene is in your part of town. It starts small, then suddenly you have a major problem on your hands. The jails are full of punks who started that way."

I resented the whole lecture, but before I could gather my thoughts to say anything, Michael piped up. "But it was only one lousy joint, and I didn't even smoke it. You talk like I committed murder."

"Shut up!" Gabe snapped. "You speak when you're spoken to, understand?" He exchanged a frown with the juvenile officer, and they gave each other quick, curt nods in agreement.

"Anyway," Michael echoed in a near whisper, "it wasn't mine."

The officer leaped on the whisper as if it were a cat burgler trying to steal away. "Whose was it? Where did you get it? Who's dealing to you punks in the barrio?"

Now Michael shut up, pressing his lips so tight they'd have to be torn apart.

"Who?"

The boy shook his head, then stared at his shoes. I can't believe what's going on, I thought. I can't believe that this is the

police station, and this is our Michael, and this red-headed
Anglo is grilling the kid like it's the crime of the century.

It went on like that for what seemed like a long, long time.
Only now that they wanted the boy to talk, he wouldn't say a
word. Finally the officer rose from his wooden chair and sighed.

"All right, Michael," he said. "We're going to release you to
the custody of your parents. But we've got your fingerprints." He
drummed his fingers on the table as if trying to make up his
mind. "If I hear one word about you in trouble again, just one
word," he warned, "I'll bring you in and then you can tell it to the
judge. Understand?"

Michael nodded grimly. We all stood, but I was too exhausted
to even sigh in relief. I felt as if it had been me hammered and
bullied for the past hour. One marijuana cigarette. Probably
every kid in town, not just in our barrio, had puffed at least one
marijuana cigarette. Why Michael?

We dragged ourselves from the room, Michael leading. The
officer put out an arm to restrain Gabe and me. "Spare the rod,"
he said ominously. I pushed past him more upset than ever. Who
the hell is he? I thought. Just who the hell?

The howls from the back bedroom tapered off. I could hear
Gabe shouting although I couldn't make out the words. I
couldn't hear Michael at all any more. Then the door slammed
and Gabe stomped out, shaking his head.

"That kid'll be the death of me," he said. He stopped in the
middle of the room and looked at me sitting there on the sofa. I
guess I still must have been crying. I hadn't even taken off my
coat yet. Then he looked at the rug and picked up the crumpled
scrap of paper, and I howled almost as loud as Michael had a few
moments earlier.

"What's the matter with you?" he said. I pointed to the scrap
of paper in his hand, and he unfolded it and read the note.
"That kid can't even write!" he hollered. "What the hell's the
matter with our schools? Kids who can't write and dope dealers
all over the playground. Jesus!"

Then he took a slower look at the note and looked at me, his
face even more grim if that's possible. "You don't have to tell
your mother," Gabe said. "Hell, you haven't talked to her in six
months."

He stuffed the paper in his trouser pocket, and his face softened. "Are you going to go?" he asked.

"No!" I said. "Not unless she's on her death bed, and even then I'd have to think about it."

* * *

Mother was born Philomena Rafa in the little adobe house across town in Los Rafas, New Mexico where Grandma and Grandpa still live. She became Philomena Baca nineteen years later when a neighboring farmer boy named Manuel Baca married her and took her away, across three cornfields and the main irrigation ditch, to the little adobe house his father and brothers had built for them.

But three fields and an irrigation ditch are no distance at all when a devoted daughter leaves her parents. With this branch of the Rafas, parents really means Mamá. The Rafas breed a powerful type of woman who, one way or another, controls the destiny of an entire family.

There were nine Rafa offspring of whom five were female. It was not until I became an adult that mysterious references to at least three other Rafas became clear. They had died in various stages of babyhood and childhood as youngsters so often did in the country in those days, although their names were revered as if they had just left the kitchen table to go out to the orchard and pick an apple.

The rivalry among the five Rafa daughters was lifelong, each trying harder than the next to be both the most dutiful daughter, that is Mamá's favorite, and the most domineering wife. Philomena had married, it turned out, a disadvantage: the young man whom all the other sisters referred to derisively as El Indio because of his dark complexion and questionable antecedents. He was a weapon with which they dutifully flogged her, diminishing her they were sure, in Grandma's eyes while telling Grandma what good daughters *they* were.

"Not pure Spanish," I remember one of my aunts saying when she thought I was out of earshot. I was fourteen at the time. It had been long enough after Mamá and Papá's marriage that normal in-laws forgave or forgot, and I was at an age when I

would look in the mirror at my own dark complexion and rail at
God for making me look like Papá.

As for the poor man himself, I conveniently forgot at the
time that only the week before I had found him in the corral
where he had gone to milk the goats, sitting among the goat
droppings and leaning against the adobe wall as he shook an
empty half pint of what had been cheap rotgut with tears streaming down his face. Was he crying because of the way his sisters-in-
law treated him? Or was it something more immediate like his
empty bottle? My romantic heart knew that he wept because they
called him El Indio as they no doubt called me La Indita.

But Mamá did not let this disadvantage keep her from the
contest. In public, at least when we children were around, she
ignored it, although she had a tendency to boss poor Papá even
harder, and he in turn, accepted it with even more than usual
meekness. After such a public incident, Mamá would beam tri-
umphantly, one of the conditions of Rafa womanhood being
fulfilled.

"Philomena is the name of a saint and a martyr," she would
often say to me after one of her sisters' most malicious assaults.
"Eventually God puts all to right. The way to heaven is not a
paved road."

But when she and Papá thought they were alone, her viper's
tongue pierced her absent sisters with a venom that would have
struck St. Philomena swiftly dead. Sisters could be called names
worse than India I learned as I listened in secret, hardly daring
to inhale for fear of being discovered.

My father would seldom answer during such attacks, unless it
was to agree when Mamá's tirades required an answer. The most
I remember him saying was, "Sí, corazón," which in English
means, more or less, "Yes, sweetheart."

When I was over at Grandma Rafa's—in our family Grandpa
Rafa was seldom mentioned, almost as if he never existed—I
would watch in fascination as the latest chapter in the contest
unreeled itself. I was so silent, so unobtrusive, that one of my
aunts, suddenly looking up and seeing me, would laugh and
refer to me in Spanish as "Quiet Big Ears," the way one might
refer to an Indian by similar names: Chief Rain-in-the-Face or
Princess Laughing Waters.

Mamá never came to my defense, which only drove the

wedge between us wider. She would look across the room, seeing perhaps the reflection of her husband, and snap at me. "Out with you! Go take care of the little ones."

Outside, in addition to smaller sister and brothers, there were cousins. And Grandpa. He always beat a retreat when the women gathered. I would follow him to the corral, or to the sluice gate of the ditch, or into the orchard, silently watching. I would piece these observations together with those of my visits here alone when neither my mother nor my aunts were around.

It was amazing. This Rafa household was not what it seemed to be. While Grandma, like her daughters, seemed to rule with her adder's tongue, she did not rule alone. On the adjacent throne, which somehow disappeared into storage when the daughters came to visit, sat the king himself who ruled by the threat of whip and fist that I never saw used. Somehow silence was his only necessary weapon, the perfect antidote for snake's venom. He used it like a virtuoso. Never had I realized the varieties and subtleties of not speaking, and he used them all. The women gathered and jousted only at his sufferance. He had no doubt given up on them long ago and tended instead to more meaningful enterprises: watering his field, currying his animals, or pruning the trees in his orchard.

As for Mamá, try as she may she never seemed to overcome the disadvantage of her marriage in seeking to become Grandma's favorite. So she turned from the things of this world to God. Especially after the population in the country grew, pointing its compass toward suburbia, and we no longer had to travel to Old Town for Sunday Mass because they built a church right in Los Rafas.

This was the perfect outlet for a Philomena. No one else's knees could be scraped so raw from kneeling on the rough floors. Of all the sisters, Mamá was the smallest, the thinnest, the boniest, so this contest was hers knees down. No one else could whisper prayers so endlessly, so audibly, while somehow keeping the volume to a level that was still a whisper. It was as if the air molecules were her allies, carrying her every hiss the full length of the church.

Then, of course, there was the Altar Society. Who else in the parish would trudge across the snow-covered fields in December, carrying an armful of spring to the crib of the Baby Jesus?

Hothouse roses were rare in Los Rafas, New Mexico, and she bore them with a tiny smile that radiated in proportion to the depth of the snow and the bite of the wind. Here, that smile seemed to say, is a miracle worthy of Juan Diego himself, bringing roses from his meeting with the Virgin of Guadalupe (courtesy of Flowers-by-Mail).

I could go on, but God, it drives me crazy just to think about it. I was the daughter who was "different," the "black sheep," who refused to set foot in church at any time other than on Sundays and holy days of obligation. Even then, what drove me to church was more superstition than belief, such was the effect that my mother's piety had on me.

She would look at my stubborn face and shake her head. "All right, honey," she would say—she would never get angry before setting off for church—"but just you wait." Then she would shake her head again and in her church-prayer whisper that I was not supposed to hear, ask herself, "Why does the same stem bear the rose and the thorn?"

I would glower at her and think to myself, "Just you wait yourself, Mamá. Just you wait.

* * *

I decided early that I didn't care if I was different. I looked at my undifferent younger brothers and sister and decided if that was what she meant, I would be different and go to hell and the hell with it!

There were five of us Rafa-Bacas. Antonio was a year younger than me, yet despite our ages we were never close. Federico was a year younger than Antonio. Then two years later came María, with finally, Manuel Junior. There had been some little creatures in between Federico and María and after Manuel, but though they made their ways into Mamá's womb, they never made their ways out alive, not even to be named. The more successful of these were stillborn, enriching Philomena's martyrdom. Each doomed little creature she transformed by faith into another shining star in her crown.

Since I was the oldest, I was the first to escape. School was the place I escaped to. In the little country school in Los Rafas there were enough children who were not Rafa-Bacas that even the most flagrant family outcast might find some kindred soul. I found several, including a few who looked at least as Indian as myself, others whose mothers were also contestants in the tournament for earthly sainthood, and not a few who only came to life when I opened the linen-worn-to-cardboard covers of books from the made-over closet that served as our school library. Cinderella was one that I remembered in particular.

At home my nose was always buried in a book. My little brothers would tease me that the printer's ink would rub off on the tip of it. They were so persistent that I would often study my face in the mirror although the stories that I read must have had something to do with it also. When I said to my reflection, "Mirror, mirror on the wall . . ." all I could see was this black spot (Was it imaginary?) on the end of this dark, large nose. In retrospect, it did take my attention away from what I considered my permanently disfigured Indian face. That had to be a blessing of some sort.

Books allowed me to escape even when I was home. My mind would be off in magic lands where the "different," the "black sheep," were the heroines. Where poor abused stepdaughters were later discovered to be true princesses.

My chorizo face would be sandwiched between stiff, hard book covers. I hardly knew what was going on around me except for brief islands of distraction, usually when Mamá screamed at me about chores or to go out into the field and find where Papá was hiding, or whatever else her fertile mind chose to worry about at the moment.

You would expect an eldest daughter to be an expert at tending to her younger siblings. I was. Sort of. I could wipe little María's snotty nose with my left hand, while turning a page with my right, not missing a single word. My voice would scream warnings and threats to an unruly Freddy about to fall into the ditch without lifting an eye off the page. I could change Manuel's soggy and smelly diaper with one hand and one eye, while still absorbed in the adventures of my printer's ink friends.

Of course I was oblivious to most of what went on around me, especially when my brothers and sister grew older and no longer came around for those driblets of motherhood that I parceled out among them. Then, as I too grew older, I stayed away from home as long as possible, feeling particularly triumphant when

high school, work, and friends left me only enough time to go
home and drop quickly to sleep.

Mamá was the jailer that any prisoner with spunk must escape. Papá was the absent creature who drifted off vaguely, usually to the corral with his goat friends, to the field where the corn
grew highest and hid best, or down the road to the cantina. My
brothers and sister were strangers whom I rarely saw and about
whom I knew less than I did about the bus schedule to town, my
friends' pet dogs, or the creatures between the covers of books.
Church was the building whose steeple I could just make out
beyond our neighbor's fields, where, if I wanted her (God forbid!), I could usually find Mamá.

It was about this time that I met Gabe, and Mamá started to
complicate my life actively.

* * *

The lights in the adobe house were out the way they always
were when I came home that night. I had him let me off near the
main road, and he walked me up the long dirt drive, over the
ditch, and past the cluster of cottonwood trees that formed an
island around which welcome cars drove to head back from the
house to the road. I kissed Gabe good night, then let myself in
the unlocked back door—you could leave doors unlocked in Los
Rafas then.

I tiptoed quietly through the kitchen, fumbling my way past
the tiny living room toward the bedroom that I shared with
María. I closed the door behind me, smiling in the dark at how
careful and clever I had been, when the room burst forth with
light. Shocked, I saw that the bed was empty. Mamá stood alongside it, her hair in curlers, and her arms folded across her chest.

"Who was that," she snapped, "sneaking you home at this
ungodly hour?"

"Nobody!"

"Don't lie to me. I know all about it."

"Then why ask me?"

Her hand answered before her sputtering words did. I defi-
antly rubbed my cheek, stubbornly determined not to cry, and
resisted the spasm of my own right hand as it raged to strike
back.

"Gabriel Padilla!" she screamed. I sensed a rustle behind the door where María must have been asleep on the sofa. "That bum! That illegitimate son of those no-good heathens from Los Barelas! What do you mean by that? Why do you disgrace me like that? I forbid you to see him again, you hear? Never again. Good God, it's probably too late already. You're already in trouble, aren't you?"

I did not dignify her outburst with an answer. She was staring with cold suspicion at my abdomen. Then she knotted her hands into fists and rushed at me, punching me in the belly like a berserk prizefighter.

"There!" she shouted after a flurry of lefts and rights. "There! That'll take care of you, you little unborn bastard!" I was too shocked to move or speak.

"Mamá!" The shout burst in from the living room. María, still dressed, threw her arms around Philomena and held on for dear life. "She's having a fit," María said. "Help me."

Still shocked by her crazy outburst, I could only stare at her saliva flecked mouth and her wild eyes as she tried to elbow herself free from María. Then Papá staggered in in his pajamas, hair disheveled, eyes groggy. Mamá started to moan like an animal, rolling her eyes so all you could see were the whites. Papá shook his head at María to let go, then gently took Mamá by the hand and led her away. Her groaning stopped immediately, and she began to cry.

"Look what we brought into the world," she said to Papá. "Just look!"

María shut the door behind them and then looked at me with terrified eyes. My younger sister, dressed in her dating clothes, had sneaked into the house after me. I thought about how Mamá had attacked me, accused me, and then I shook my head at María. It was so bizarre that I started to laugh hysterically. I didn't even feel where Mamá had punched me.

"You're as crazy as she is," María said. Then she quickly undressed just in case, I suppose, Mamá should return and realize that María too had been out late, God knows where doing God knows what.

María dropped into bed and fell asleep almost immediately. It was a long time before I calmed down enough to undress and even longer before I slipped under the covers beside my sister.

Confused, I thought about packing up and leaving right then. But where would I go, especially at this hour of the night? My mind was in a turmoil as I lay rigid beside María. In a way I felt that I was awake forever, but then, almost in an instant it seemed, dawn lifted the dark from the room but not from my heart.

I listened to the rest of the household shuffling and bumping about while beside me María snored the peaceful sleep of the innocent. Even the alarm clock did not penetrate her dreams. Once again I considered packing and leaving through the window. Then the smell of breakfast sneaked through my defenses, and sullenly I rose and dressed.

When I tiptoed from the room I saw Mamá kneeling in the living room before the statue of the Virgin with its lighted votive. Her eyes were closed, her hands clasped together beseechingly, and her lips moved imperceptibly, at odds with the loudness of her whisper.

I didn't listen. I couldn't stomach it. I rushed past to the kitchen where the table was already set and Papá and my brothers were eating like pigs as if nothing had happened. Papá pulled a plate hot from the oven and set it at an empty place.

"Philomena made this especially for you," he said.

I looked at the scrambled eggs with green chili and felt an urge to throw up. She's put something in mine, I thought. Some witches' brew to cleanse what her fists imagined they had pounded to death.

I almost gagged as I spoke. "No thanks, Papá. I just have time to stop by church on the way to school."

Papá's face brightened as he nodded, his mouth full of flour tortilla. "Mamá will like that," he said after a gulp and a swallow.

Of course I didn't go to church. I took the early bus to town and stopped across from school for a cup of coffee and an order of French fries, eating them slowly and deliberately with the calm faith that they were not seasoned with aborticide. Henceforth, I knew, I would eye Mamá's food with the same suspicion that I eyed cokes offered by certain boys who had so little faith that they relied on the powers of Spanish fly rather than on their own charms, and I would wish that I had been born of royal blood so I could extend my forefinger carelessly and a taster would leap to the table and take the first bite.

I ached all through the school morning. My soul was a tooth with an incurable cavity. The teacher in my favorite English class asked me questions at least three or four times with eyebrows arched, more to leash in my straying attention than to test my knowledge.

When an office monitor tiptoed into math carrying a message to the teacher who called my name, I panicked, wondering what I had done now. I dragged to the office where an impatient clerk told me I was to hurry to the emergency room at St. Joseph's Hospital. They could not find my father at work, and I had been referred to as next of kin. That was all she knew, and my panic turned to ice-water dread.

I stood by the exit from the bus staring out the window but seeing nothing. I rushed into the hospital, looking for the emergency room, and saw in the lobby my Aunt Bertha who rushed up to me with a wild look on her face that was capped by uncombed hair standing almost straight up.

"I think she's coming out of the ether now," Aunt Bertha said. "They'll let us in in a minute." Then she started to emote, but I couldn't understand a word she said, not even who *she* was who was coming out of the ether. It was a regular aria by the fat soprano, and I wondered why it was that we New Mexicans hadn't invented opera instead of the Italians. But through my own panic I realized that it must be Mamá because if it had been any other next of kin, Mamá would have been in the lobby singing a duet with my aunt.

In a short while a tight-faced little nun walked briskly up and nodded for us to follow. Philomena was sitting up in bed, holding out her right hand that had ballooned into a white mass of plaster from fingertips to wrist. She looked like a priest with a holy water sprinkler ready to bless the congregation. It was the same hand that had tried to deliver a knockout blow to my insides.

"She's been calling for you," Aunt Bertha whispered.

Guilt, I said to myself. When I looked at Mamá she was staring at me as if she had been watching me ever since we had come into the room. A strange look of recognition flashed between us, then the tears started streaming down her cheeks.

"My baby," Philomena whined, "my first born."

I looked at Aunt Bertha who had a beatific glow on her face. I saw that I was trapped. For one of the few times in my young life I did what circumstance and other people's expectations demanded. I rushed to the bed and threw my arms around Mamá, avoiding that white boxing glove.

"What happened?" I asked in a falsely quavering voice.

I had visions of God aiming a forefinger at her and spearing that offending right hand. Or a statue of the Virgin Mary falling from its niche and onto her hand when she tried to catch it. But it was nothing so dramatic. She and Bertha had just arrived at the supermarket in Bertha's car. As they alighted, Mamá had somehow left her hand in the door and slammed it shut. The bones were a mess, and the doctor said her hand might never be the same.

The three of us joined our teary voices in the trio from "The Martyr of Los Rafas." Those few times when I looked at Mamá and our eyes met, I could see a hidden message as if each of us knew what the other was thinking but dared not say it. Out loud I assured her that her injury pained me more than it pained her—which it didn't.

For all of that, she never once said to me that she was sorry for last night. Finally, in total submission to hypocrisy, and perhaps hoping that the words would be mother to the wish, I said, "I'm so sorry, Mamá." She gave me a self-righteous nod of her head and blink of eyes, interpreting what I was sorry for in her own way (Gabriel Padilla no doubt).

Years later I would look at what that right hand became, a little chicken claw of limited ability, and the whole thing would come back to me. I would remember how she never said she was sorry then or since, preferring instead to act it out in her own way.

*   *   *

The front door slammed, and I heard the weak-batteried cough of the starter on the pickup truck. I blinked in surprise because I hadn't heard Gabe say goodbye, although I knew he must be going to the construction site up in the heights. He was building us a new house, away from the barrio, on a lot we had scraped and saved for and finally made the down payment on five years ago when I went to work as a bookkeeper for an insurance broker. The construction business was slow now, and Gabe was using the slack time to finish our own place.

I sat still and listened. It was so quiet, not like what I remembered from my parents' house while I was growing up. I strained to hear any signs of life in the boys' bedroom. Not a peep. I sat still a moment longer before I took off my coat. Calmer now, I picked up the telephone and called my boss to tell him that I wouldn't be back this afternoon—family emergency.

For the longest while I stood outside Michael's door, not so much listening as trying to decide whether or not to go in and what I'd say if I entered. I thought with resentment about that red-faced cop bullying my boy. Then I thought about Michael's stubborn antagonism to the cop and my gnawing doubt about whether or not this one marijuana cigarette was the tip of the iceberg or just a stupid kid stunt except that this particular stupid kid was unlucky enough to get caught.

Little Michael, deliberately conceived in love in contrast to Junior, who was more or less unplanned but whom Gabe and I loved equally.

Then I thought of love gone sour, of Philomena. It was strange. One does not choose her mother or father. Or brothers or sisters. Or even her children. We only choose our mates. The others come to us uninvited in whatever way they, not we, want. But how well we live seems to depend more on what we do with what we do *not* choose than on what we *do* choose.

I tapped lightly on the door, leaning forward to listen. "Go away!" the tearful voice shouted.

"I need to talk to you, Michael."

"Leave me alone!"

I opened the door cautiously and stepped inside. He was huddled in the lower of the bunk beds, his scuffed tennis shoes hanging over the edge. All I could think was how he had outgrown the bed, and I felt remorse for not having the money to buy one that fit him better.

"Are you all right?"

He glowered at me belligerently. I realized that he wasn't my baby anymore and hadn't been for a long time. That parents have to get used to looks that could kill. After a moment or two he wiped at his eyes with the back of his hand and looked out the window.

"I didn't do anything," Michael finally said. He turned away from the window and gave me the hate stare again.

"Your father and I—"

He thrust his head forward like a charging beast. "That damned bully!" he shouted. "You're the one who said you didn't believe in people hitting other people and look what you let him do to me!"

For an instant I felt like going over and slapping his face for talking that way. Then I saw the look of fright flash through his eyes, and I realized that he was just a scared kid.

"You know how the police watch the boys here in the barrio."

"Yeah! If you've got a dark complexion. Otherwise they don't give a damn what you do!"

He turned his face from me again, staring out the window, pressing his lips tight together. "Are there any gangs at school?" I asked. I couldn't imagine the nuns at St. Mary's putting up with any such nonsense. The twisted smile he flicked at me mirrored his agreement: What a stupid question.

"I worry about you, Michael." I said. "I know what can happen around here. Some of these kids are on the fast track to jail—or worse."

But it was obvious that I wasn't getting anywhere. He turned away and walled himself off. A parade of fears started to march through my mind to the tune of "La Cucaracha," the insidious hiss of maracas like the warning of a snake, the marchers thrusting their hips left and right in obscene gyrations as they looked back over their shoulders at me and leered.

"I can't stand this, Michael!" I cried, hating myself for losing control. "You've got to tell me what's going on!"

He turned back, his face hard and Indian-like, a mirror of my own. "Have I ever been in trouble before?" he said, expecting no answer because we both already knew that the answer was no. "You know all my friends. Are any of them gangsters?" No again.

But logic is a feeble weapon against imagination. I could see the terrifying outcome from the fatal marijuana cigarette. Secret meetings in dark alleys. Furtive laughter in the quiet dark. Hidden packets passed from hand to hand. Cigarette papers traded for syringes and needles. The police. The judge. Prison. Death. The grave. Hell. Eternity.

"But why, Michael?" I pleaded. "I just don't understand."

He stared out the window as if he hadn't heard me. Did *he* understand? I thought.

"You've never done anything like this before," I said.

Nothing. Not even a blink. I became angry again at his stubborn refusal to answer.

"Well, you know what your father said. Straight home from school from now on. You're grounded until we come to some understanding about this. You're lucky it isn't worse."

His eyes twitched a trace of a pucker as if he were fighting back tears. Then dry eyed, he snapped his head toward me. "It's your fault!" he hissed in that hateful voice that terrifies me. "It's heredity," he said, stabbing the hate deeper and twisting it. "I'm just like your family, and there's nothing I can do about it."

I was crying again from anger and frustration and guilt. I was staring toward that hateful voice, but I couldn't see a thing. I whirled around and left the room, slamming the door. Let him sulk in his prison, the ungrateful little wretch. Let him give in to his genes and his family history. It's a hell of a great excuse.

"Ma!" The surprised voice greeted me as Junior reached back to keep the front door from slamming. "You're home early, Ma. Is there anything to eat in this dump?"

I wiped at my cheeks and tried to calm my voice. "There are those apples that your father brought from Grandma Padilla's."

He made a face, then blinked alert as if he had finally really seen me. "What's the matter, Ma?"

I shook my head. "You left the front door unlocked when you went out," I said. But my heart wasn't in my nagging.

"Did you get my note? Are we going?"

"Go in the kitchen," I said. "If you don't want apples, get some milk."

*　*　*

We no more choose our children than we do our mothers. When the mother I had not chosen was released from the hospital with her mending chicken claw, she found her dutiful black sheep keeping everyone somewhat fed and almost as clean-clothed as usual. The only things that had changed were the noise level and the prayer level.

The minute Philomena walked in the door, the noise and

prayer levels rose as if a beehive had been irritated—the queen
bee had returned. Oh, such claw wringing bids for sympathy. It
was enough to drive you to murder.

If there had been the slightest doubt about Gabriel Padilla
before, it was drowned by Mamá's tears and bids for sympathy.
Maybe what I was really wishing was just to be away from home,
which in my naivete I mistook for love.

"Let's run away and get married," I said to Gabe one night
when I was more than normally distraught about Philomena.
"We could drive to El Paso, cross the border into Juárez, and be
married like that."

He looked up startled when I snapped my fingers. "We have
to finish school," he said. I didn't want to hear that. "I'd have to
borrow my brother's car—if he'd let us use it." I didn't want to
hear that either. "Then," and here he looked away with pain,
"what about my mother?" The last thing I wanted to hear about
was his widowed mother. So logical. So damnably, irritably sensible. Just like a man.

"And besides," he went on, "I need a job that pays a lot more
than busing dishes part-time." It was like the pounding of the
last nail in the coffin, of the judge's gavel as he pronounced
sentence.

The next six months waiting for school to be over seemed to
take forever. I can't think of another six-month period in my life
that dragged so slowly except during my difficult second pregnancy.

When graduation approached we got caught up in the excitement. "No more pencils, no more books, no more teachers' dirty
looks." We were getting ready to step out into the adult world,
and wasn't it about time? Gabe and I scrimped on dates, and he
used the money to buy a class ring. It was to be my wedding ring,
which somehow seemed very appropriate.

We kept the secret from everyone except Gabe's brother, who
was going to be best man (and who had the car), and my friend,
Celia Gonzales, who was to be maid-of-honor. Instead of driving
to Juárez, we found a Justice of the Peace, a distant cousin of
Gabe's, in the little town of Corrales just a few miles away.

Of course, that was the ultimate breech with Philomena. I
didn't think about it at the time. I was too excited about becom-

ing Mrs. Gabriel Padilla. The only other time I felt that exultation was when our two sons came forth from my body, but with those miracles there was the pain, and there was no pain in becoming Mrs. Gabriel Padilla.

The Justice of the Peace was appropriately solemn and dignified as if we were real adults. When Gabe put the class ring on my finger, I turned it around with my thumb so the face of the ring was on the inside of my finger, and it looked like a real wedding ring. Gabe's brother had a bottle of California champagne, and we sat in the parked car outside the JP's adobe house and drank to the future of our marriage. We were still guzzling the last of the wine from the paper cups when the lights in the JP's house went out, and we figured it was time to move on.

We drove back to Albuquerque, stopping at one of the clubs on the west side to have something to drink. The waiter looked at Gabe and me with a jaundiced eye and would not serve us.

"But we're married," Gabe kept insisting, holding up my hand to show him the ring. No dice.

So we had a coke and then drove Celia home and Gabe's brother home and took off alone in the car. "What'll we do?" Gabe asked. We were heading north from Barelas toward the center of town.

It wasn't what you think. All of the eighteen years of my life there had been mamá's curfew which dragged me down like a ball and chain. Even when I sneaked in past curfew time, the guilt hung heavy so I didn't enjoy being out late.

"Let's go to the midnight movie," I said. "Then we can go to our motel and watch the late late show on TV. We can stay up all night. We don't have to answer to anybody! We're married!"

Gabe thought it was a pretty neat idea too. So we spent our wedding night trying to keep our eyes open. There was no consummation in the usual way. You might say our marriage was consummated in sleepy laughter watching reruns of old TV sitcoms.

To tell the truth, Mamá had never told me a thing, and all the gym teachers talked about at school was the shame of venereal disease which was, I thought, some slightly escalated version of the heartbreak of psoriasis. Where babies came from I wasn't sure, even though we had always had chickens and goats at home. Somehow it had something to do with drinking from dirty glasses or French kissing, and I was particularly careful about both those things that night.

Gabe and I can laugh about it now. But Gabe didn't know much more than I did back then, and he was relieved when the dawn came up with test patterns on the TV screen. We were both too droopy eyed to do anything but crawl into bed with our clothes still on.

The maid's knock woke us up about noon, and we hurried out because we didn't want to pay for another day. We stopped at Bernalillo for breakfast, praying that it would fortify us for the ordeal of telephoning home. Philomena started screaming at me right away, escalating to hysteria after I said "married." There was no getting through to her after that. Finally I hung up on her in exasperation.

Gabe had better luck with his mother. His brother had already been over there and told her, and she asked for me and told me how wonderful she thought it was. She was looking forward to seeing us when we got back from Santa Fe.

We moved in with Gabe's mother, and she made me feel at home like I had never felt before. But Philomena was another matter. She would telephone during the day, waking Widow Padilla who was working nights, and spuming curses at her for stealing me away. Then she'd call in the middle of the night to be sure I was home from work, giving me her midnight message. I was living in sin, she said. We hadn't been married by a priest so it was no marriage at all.

Then one Saturday afternoon there was a knock on the front door. I was alone and busy in the kitchen. It took me awhile to wipe my hands and straighten my dress and answer. Whoever had knocked was no longer there. I looked up and down the narrow road—it was more like an alley—but could see nothing. I hadn't heard a car, so I thought it must have been one of the neighbors.

Then I heard a knock at the back out by the corral. "Just a minute!" I yelled, hurrying through the small house. When I opened the door, there she was.

"My baby!" Philomena said in her most saccharine voice, reaching out to embrace me.

"Mamá!"

"What have they done to you?" she asked, clutching onto me tightly. "I was ready to call the police to tell them you had been kidnapped." She tugged at me, trying to pull me out the door, but I planted my feet firmly and held my ground. "I waited until they were both out of the house," she said, "then I hurried up before any of the neighbors saw me."

I had not quite wiggled loose, and I really didn't want to hurt her, but her insistent hanging on began to panic me. I looked down my arm and saw the little chicken claw clutching feebly and something inside of me snapped.

"Let go of me, Mamá!"

When I pulled away roughly—she wouldn't have let go otherwise—her hands raised up in surprise, then reached out beseechingly toward my face as if she wanted to take hold of it and kiss it.

"I just want to take my baby home," she said.

I backed away, angry now. "I'm a married woman. I'm here of my own free will. I don't want to go."

Her eyes narrowed, and her expression chilled. She tossed her head, motioning in the direction of the corral and the rest of the closely packed little adobe houses. "It stinks!" she said. "This is a pigsty. A sewer. That's all you'll ever get from these trashy Padillas. You might as well be living in a hogan."

"Leave, Mamá. Please leave."

"You're no daughter of mine!" she screamed. Her face contorted in anger as she shook her chicken claw at me. "We found you on the doorstep!" she shouted. A cruel smile flashed at me and her eyes gleamed. "Just a little Indian baby some dirty squaw wanted to get rid of."

"Good!" I shouted back. "I'm glad!" I shoved her out and slid the bolt shut. I leaned against the door, feeling the feeble pounding of her fists, and I cried. "You're not my mother," I whispered. "You're not. You're not."

* * *

You'd think that chapter of my life was closed forever. The way the story is supposed to end is that the young newlyweds move far away, someplace like California, out of the clutches of suffocating family love. But there was Gabe's mother to whom he felt an obligation. When I mentioned California, Gabe said,

"This is our home. Our roots are here. There are generations of us, including my father, planted in the old cemetary. Nobody's going to drive me away from my home." He meant Philomena.

Don't get me wrong. It wasn't bad living with Mamá Padilla. She was a sweet woman, a quiet woman, who showed her love by what she did, not by what she said or demanded. All three of us worked, she as a nurse's aide at St. Joseph's Hospital, Gabe as an apprentice carpenter, and me at the dime store. We all shared what had to be done at home. It wasn't at all like two young people living with a parent.

I was the outcast from my own family now, at least as far as Philomena was concerned. Gabe and I might join uneasy family truces at holidays, but I hated every minute of it. Somehow I had less to say to my father, who just seemed to drift farther away, cut loose from his moorings. I saw my sister and brothers occasionally, though it was less than we saw Gabe's brother. What I remember most were Philomena's illnesses. I measured my encounters with Philomena by the visits to the hospital.

* * *

Philomena's hysterectomy was the first mutilation. It really started the summer before she went to the hospital—actually before she even went to the doctor to find out what was wrong.

One night Gabe was at a union meeting and Mamá Padilla was working the night shift. I was going to take a good soak in the tub, put on my pajamas, and just do luxurious nothing for the rest of the evening when, of course, there was a knock on the door. This is a barrio where people don't open their doors at night until they've pulled aside the curtains and peeked out. It was hard to see in the dark. This was over fifteen years ago, and they still don't have street lights in that part of town.

All I could tell was that it was a man. I had decided that I wasn't going to open and was ready to let the curtains drop, when he stepped to the door again. In the feeble light I recognized my brother, Antonio, a grim expression on his face, and I went to let him in. He looked over his shoulder furtively, then entered as if he were hiding from someone.

"Well, Tony," I said. "Long time no see."

"She hasn't been talking to you, has she?" I wasn't sure if he meant some irate girl friend or Philomena or who, but I shook my head anyway. His tight face and strained eyes relaxed a little as we moved from the door to the little front room.

Even when I insisted, he would not sit down. He paced the few steps across, then the few steps back from one adobe wall to the other. I sat on the lumpy sofa waiting for him to say something. He hadn't responded to a few of my remarks, and I was damned annoyed. You don't see somebody for weeks, then they walk in on you and clam up.

After a few laps he started talking although he didn't look at me or stop pacing. He threw the words at the wall, whichever one he happened to be facing at the moment, as if they were rubber balls that would find their way back to me—whether in a high bounce or a low dribble didn't matter.

"You sure she hasn't been talking to you?"

"Who?"

Then a couple of more laps, and he stopped in the middle of the room and looked around as if he had suddenly found himself there and was surprised. "Is anybody here?"

"Just me."

He started pacing again. "I'm leaving," he said, and I thought: It's about time. "Leaving home," he explained.

I wasn't too keen on playing twenty questions so I just kept quiet. I kept thinking about a warm bath and about my damp pajamas rolled up on the ironing board in the kitchen waiting to be ironed.

"Did you hear me?" he said. "I'm leaving home."

I nodded. He had to mean Philomena's. He wasn't married, and I don't think he had moved in with anybody.

"Are you sure she hasn't been talking to you? She says you phone her twice a week. Every Tuesday and Friday."

Well. That was pretty funny, and I couldn't help but laugh. That did it. He stopped right in the middle of the room and looked at me.

"Jesus save me," I said. Then I noticed that strange look on his face, and I started to get worried. Was he drunk or high on drugs?

"What does that mean?" he asked. "She used to come over on

the two o'clock bus to visit you every Monday and Wednesday. She kept us all up-to-date on what you were doing."

"This is crazy," I said. "I haven't seen Philomena since Christmas. You were in the room the whole time. You know we didn't say more than a dozen words to each other."

He stood in the middle of the room transfixed. It was as if all the motion had frozen solid. He even looked like ice. Then his face clouded, and he suddenly burst into tears.

"What kind of world is it when you can't even believe your own mother?" he cried. Tears were streaming down his face. "She takes my paycheck every Friday," he said. "That's so I won't go out and get drunk on Saturday night. Then she makes me go to six o'clock Mass with her on Sundays. 'No twelve o'clock drunkards' Mass for you,' she says. If I don't go with her, I don't get my allowance on Monday morning.

"Are you sure you don't phone her Tuesdays and Fridays? She said you were three months pregnant, and that she and Papá would be grandparents soon."

I knew Tony wasn't too smart, but this beat all. It really got under my skin, and I was mad. "Damn it!" I said. "What does she mean telling those lies about me? I'm not pregnant. I never see her except when the family gets together for Thanksgiving and Christmas."

The flow of tears stopped, and his eyes widened in amazement. His head started to shake, but I didn't know whether it was in disbelief or whether he was out of control and trembling.

"Now you know why I have to leave," he finally said. "I don't know where I am with that crazy woman."

"Where are you going?"

"San Francisco."

It was my turn to be amazed. I never knew Tony had it in him. I thought I was the only rebel in the family. "My friend and I are taking the Greyhound tomorrow morning first thing." Then he frowned and stared at me silently for awhile. "Are you sure she hasn't been talking to you?"

"For God's sakes, no!"

"Well, whatever she says, don't believe her." Then he stepped up to me and grabbed my upper arms and gave me a quick kiss on the forehead. "Adiós, sis. Have you got some extra cash you can lend me? Until I get settled? I'll write you from the Golden Gate."

I didn't think twice about it. I went for my purse and pressed some limp bills into his hand—I had been saving for this real cute dress I had seen downtown at Lerner's—and gave him a peck on the cheek. He gave me a weak grin, then turned and left. It all happened so quickly that for awhile I didn't believe it. I thought maybe I had had a hallucination. Until I looked at the purse in my hand with the secret compartment that was now empty, and I thought: I'll never see that money again.

Of course you know who got in touch with me the very next day. At work yet. She must have telephoned and wakened poor Mamá Padilla, then hopped on the bus that stopped right in front of Woolworth's.

"There you are!" this irritating, familiar voice spat at me. I rang the cash register and stapled the receipt to the folded over top of the bag and handed it to the customer. "Don't pretend you don't hear me," Philomena said. The customer gave her a funny look, grabbed her package and her change, and walked off in a hurry, looking back over her shoulder as she hit the door.

"It's your fault," she said, "that your baby brother has run away."

"Hello, Mamá," I said, as calmly as I could. "What brings you to town?"

That stopped her—for about the blink of an iguana's eye. "If you hadn't set an example by running away and marrying that dirty Padilla, he'd never have thought of it. Where did Tony get the money to leave home?"

"Mamá!" I hissed. "Be quiet. The customers are looking." Then I added in a whisper, "I don't know what you're talking about."

Customers weren't about to deter Philomena. I was afraid that my supervisor would hear the ruckus and come over and then I'd be out looking for another job.

"The cookware is this way," I said in a loud, clear voice. Then I started toward the section where there were no people.

But once you get chewing gum on your shoe you can't get it off. Philomena was going at me as we walked down the aisle. "What did he say to you?" she insisted. "What did Tony say?"

"I never saw him."

"What have people been saying about him? You shouldn't believe what people say."

"Nothing," I said, stopping in front of the aluminum coffee pots that were on sale this week. "I never talk to Tony."

The whirlwind died down for a moment because I guess she believed me. "He ran off with Angel Romero," she finally said, as if that should be of significance.

"So?" I didn't even know Angel Romero.

"Well, don't believe anything anybody tells you," she said. "And if he should get in touch with you, tell him he broke his mother's heart."

Then she turned and click-clicked her way toward the exit, stopping halfway down the counter to look back. "Don't neglect your poor old Mamá," she said in a quavering voice. "Your Mamá loves you, no matter what." Then she was gone.

When I told Gabe about it that evening, he just shook his head, flicked the upper half of the evening paper to cover his face, and reached for his can of beer. He didn't even say boo. He didn't need to. I could tell by the look on his face that he thought it was just more of Philomena's craziness, and he had had enough of that to last a lifetime. He didn't know Angel Romero, or at least he didn't admit to it.

I had only received one postcard from Tony, showing a cable car on a steep hill, before Philomena went to the hospital. Obviously, the money he owed me wasn't attached, but then I had already kissed that goodbye. I never made any connection between Tony's departure and Philomena's surgery except in some vague way. It must have been a few years later when I was watching television (we finally scraped up the down payment and got in hock for one) that everything came together.

It was the ten o'clock network news. The dishes were done and our then baby Michael was in his crib. I was pooped and turned on the dumb thing although I really wasn't paying attention until the newscaster mentioned San Francisco. The cameras showed a marching crowd of protestors, signs in hand, banners stretched across their path. There on one end of a banner I saw Tony. I know it was him. A cold chill jolted me as my eyes came alive and read the words on the banner: "Gay rights!"

I turned to Gabe who was on the sofa beside me. He was

looking at me and just nodded his head. "The one next to him holding his hand is Angel Romero," he said.

I didn't believe what I saw, so I looked back at the screen but Tony was gone although there were more of the same banners and signs. I felt dizzy and sick to my stomach. When I looked back at Gabe he was still watching me with concern.

"I didn't see any point in telling you," he said. "There was nothing you could do about it. It's his life."

* * *

The other things that happened over the years were much simpler. Or let's say that they were easier for me to understand. My brother Freddy and my sister María just followed in the family footsteps. In this case it was my father's side of the family, since they took to the bottle like babies to a nipple.

What this meant was that Freddy wasn't able to hold a job for long, and he would show up at the door with a beard, disheveled clothes, and an aroma that would shame a goat. What he wanted was money. "Bus fare," he'd say. Then he's ask for pretty expensive bus fare—enough for a trip to Gallup which was about the same as for a fifth of rotgut. Other times, like the annual family gatherings at Thanksgiving and Christmas, he'd be neat and clean and sober as a nun going to confession.

María was another matter. Not only did she keep up with Freddy and Papá when it came to drinking, like a loyal daughter she also tried to make up for Tony. I never did get it straight whether she actually married them or not. And I had only met one of them, a dark Navajo who owned a tourist trading post on the U.S. highway. What I did not miss were the little bundles that eventually found their way to Grandma's house where Philomena would avidly take them over.

These little bundles from heaven contributed only minor ravages to Philomena's martyrdom. A scalded hand from an encounter with a formula sterilizer. A hand that, unfortunately, never did completely heal, and in conjunction with her chicken claw, left her almost incapable of grasping and holding. Opossum eyes from interrupted sleep. Back problems from bending over and lifting babies.

Yet these infirmities, as I said, were tempered by the thrill of little creatures to fuss over and mold, so that they were but minor afflictions until her back became a permanent problem. That required the removal of a disk and a surrender of baby lifting to someone else. I don't think it was María. Producing babies might be fun, but birthing them and caring for them were other matters.

The big problem at this time turned out to be Manuel, Junior, the baby of the family. Manny did not take after his father or his brother. He set off on a self-destructive course all his own.

I suppose he had been doing what he was doing since early in Gabe's and my marriage—Manny was eight years younger than me. He was at that crazy age then, and those were those crazy times when anything you did seemed to be all right.

I was busy with Michael, and since I only saw the family on holidays, I did not know what was going on. In retrospect it was easy to see that Manny got no help at all from Papá, Freddy, or María. For them it was party-time forever. Break open the bottle.

I don't know exactly what Philomena was up to then. I mean I know what she was up to generally—the same old thing. But I didn't know what she was up to specifically except maybe retreating to baby-care with María's little bundles for home. It was always easier to take care of babies or pets. They don't talk back. They worship the sight and sound of you; they coo or wag their tails when you acknowledge them. A few diapers, a wet paper with a little caca on it, a bottle, an occasional bowl of scraps. It's easy. Until the babies grow up. Pets never do.

Gabe and I were having an argument one night about what Michael was going to be when he grew up (he was three years old then). I was in the early stages of pregnancy with Gabriel Junior and prone to hysteria over things like that. I was working myself up to the teary stage when there was a knock on the door.

"Hi, sis. Mamá kicked me out."

There he was, the skinny little ferret, with his shifty eyes moving back and forth. He was dressed in those outrageous cholo clothes that I hated: light tan chinos and a plaid shirt buttoned at the collar. He stood ramrod straight, as if he had inherited Philomena's fused spine. He walked in with that strange, insolent walk that went with the costume. His back was straight as if a steel rod went through it, although his shoulders leaned back a bit so it looked as if he were sneaking up on somebody. His knees rose high like a marionette moved by strings. His shoulders and arms barely moved at all, while his head bobbed up and down as if it were taking the measure of you and knew a secret about you that you were ashamed of.

Gabe had been standing in the middle of the living room glaring at me. Now he went over to the TV and turned it on and flopped onto the sofa. Manny's little lizard eyes kept moving back and forth like he was following a fly that was circling nearer and nearer.

"Sit down," I said.

"Can I stay here for a little while?" Manny asked. "Until I get things straightened out?"

What things? I thought.

The things, he told us, were Philomena. Looking back, I realize he knew my soft spot only too well. She was crazier than ever, he said, pouring all she had onto those captive little grand-babies of hers. That made me jealous. What had Philomena done for our little Michael? Which was crazy of me. Here I had cut myself off from her—disowned her really—and I was jealous because she wasn't spoiling my baby son.

It's a wonder I didn't ask my husband to let Manny stay here permanently. Of course he could stay awhile. Poor brother. He could have the sofa all to his own—when TV time was over. It was only later that I regretted my family loyalty.

It didn't start out so bad—a telephone call from the high school. The ring woke Mamá Padilla; the rest of us were gone. In her half sleep she thought they were calling about Gabe, and she didn't understand.

"I'm calling about Manuel Baca," the officious voice said in crisp Anglo tones. "We haven't seen him for two weeks, and we wondered if he was sick."

"I don't know Manuel Baca," Mamá Padilla said, forgetting our recent addition to the sofa.

Then after a few more of the same exchanges, as if saying the same thing over again and louder would make someone under-stand, Mamá Padilla realized what it was all about. "You want my daughter-in-law," she said. "She's at work."

So Mamá telephoned me at work, and I in turn telephoned the school. Sick? of course not, I said. Then I told the attendance lady that I would come by on my lunch break.

Playing hookey was no big deal as far as I was concerned. My husband felt differently about it. He thought school was sacred. But it didn't bother me too much, and I hardly listened to Manny's lies about changing his classes, and the teachers confusing him with another student with the same name, and a whole bunch more. I even believed him when he said he would get right back to school the very next day.

What started to get me were the mysterious telephone calls at all hours. Strange voices would be at the other end of the line at two o'clock in the morning, croaking out a cryptic, "¿Cucaracha?"

When I'd spit out in anger, "Who the hell is this?", they'd hang up.

When Manny was there, he'd be on the telephone so much I thought it was growing out of his ear. He'd always turn his back to me, whisper quickly into the mouthpiece, then listen awhile before he dropped the receiver.

Then one day I saw a car parked down the dirt road with two men sitting in it smoking and talking. This didn't seem too strange, except that this was a narrow road and people seldom parked their cars there for long because no one else could get though. So, they're just there for a little while, I thought. But they were there for three days in a row. One night Gabe and I came home late from a movie, and there was that car with the glowing tips of two cigarettes showing in the dark.

We were getting ready for bed when there was a rattle at the back door. Gabe and I looked at each other, then he rebuttoned his shirt and went to see what it was.

"Don't turn on the light," came the whisper from the kitchen. It was Manny.

The spring on the sofa sighed, then Gabe came in with a scowl on his face. "This can't go on," he said.

"What?"

He looked at me as if trying to figure out what to say. "Manny," he finally said.

Then there was a knock on the front door. Not a rattle. Not a quiet knock. But not a door-buster either. Just a firm "Let me in; I know you're there" knock.

"Jesus Christ!" Gabe said, heading toward the front door with fire in his eyes.

This time I heard other movement in the house. I hoped it wasn't Mamá Padilla or Michael. That's all we needed.

"Manuel Baca?" this authoritative voice asked. Before Gabe could explain, the voice went on. "I have a warrant for the arrest of Manuel Baca. You'd better let me in."

I turned my head toward the sofa in the other room as if I could see through the wall. I knew what that other movement was now. Then I heard a familiar squeak. Heavy footsteps rushed into the house, and the authoritative voice spat out toward the kitchen—the other man must have been in back—"He's going out the window!"

They never caught him. Manny knew the neighborhood better than they did, especially in the dark. We sat up waiting for whatever was going to happen to happen. Finally we both fell asleep sitting on the sofa. The officers never came back that night.

During all of those weeks that Manny lived with us, Philomena never once telephoned. The very next morning though, while we were having breakfast, you just know who called.

"What have you done to my baby?" she whined at me. I was in no mood, I tell you. It didn't take more than another two sentences before I hung up on her.

That was when the two officers came back to talk to us. It made me late for work which was the final straw. I was about ready for a screaming fit. They kept asking these questions about Manny's friends and where he went and a whole lot more that we didn't know. They wouldn't tell us a thing. When they left they said that if he ever showed up again we should report him—sure, I thought—or we were liable to get into trouble for harboring a criminal.

I don't know how I got through that day. Philomena telephoned me at work twice, and I hung up on her both times. The last time at least she didn't ask me what I had done to her baby. Instead she said, "How could he do this to me?" I was more concerned about what he was doing to himself, but never mind.

A week later they caught him cruising down Rafas Road in a low rider heading for Philomena's. I saw Philomena an extra time that year when we met in Juvenile Court. It was more than I could stand, and I'm sure that was the reason that Gabriel, Junior was born six weeks early and had such a hard time at first.

For awhile I was afraid the poor baby wasn't going to make it.

That was the last I saw of Manny. I only heard about him after that. They sent him to reform school for dealing dope. After that he was out for awhile, then back in. Only this time it was state prison. He wasn't a juvenile anymore. Finally one day they found him in a flop house over on the wrong side of town dead from a heroin overdose. Poor Manny. It was then that Philomena had her second stroke. She had the first one when they sent him to jail the first time.

                              *   *   *

Now you know what Michael meant by heredity. Maybe if I was some kind of professor I could explain it all. Then I could either accept the fact that that's the way it is and Michael is doomed, or I could tell the kid what I really think: That it's just an excuse. Nothing is fixed. There's something in the world called evolution; at least that's what they told me back when I was in school. Now shape up and get on with it.

I didn't telephone Philomena back that afternoon. I wasn't ready. After an hour or so Gabe came back from the construction site wound up so tight I thought he was going to explode.

"Let's get out town," he said. "I can't stand this place."

So we packed up the boys and drove up the Pan American Freeway to Santa Fe. We didn't stop at Gabe's cousin's this time but rented two rooms in one of those little old motels on the outskirts of town, one for the boys and another for us. The privacy was absolute luxury.

The next morning, Sunday, all four of us went to the cathedral. We arrived a little early so Gabe could stop by the side chapel where they keep the statue of La Conquistadora whom he calls Our Lady of New Mexico. Then we went into the main part of the church for Mass.

I thought maybe we would be lucky and have services by the Archbishop himself. He, like us, is Spanish flavored by a hint of the Pueblos. It used to anger me that it took over a hundred and twenty years for the Church to wise up and stop sending us all those Anglo bishops that they sent ever since our great-great-grandparents became Americans at gunpoint. But God is color-blind, and some of the Anglo priests and nuns that I've known were just like us even though they couldn't speak our langauge.

I was disappointed when the Archbishop did not appear. Instead it was a pale-faced little man with thinning hair the color of dirty straw who, when he made his announcements in a thick brogue, sounded as if he had just stepped off the boat from the old country.

Snatches of the sermon registered on me from time to time. When he said, "whosoever shall smite thee on thy right cheek, turn to him the other also," I felt a rise of anger because all that ever got me was another smack in the face.

When I heard "if thy right eye offend thee, pluck it out," I suddenly thought of my mother; she's crazy enough to do just that. And "If thy right hand offend thee, cut it off, and cast it from thee," brought back memories of Philomena's chicken claw of a hand.

I started to feel sad, especially because the brogue reminded me of an old parish priest of ours who always spoke with great longing about going back before he died to see his old mother in Ireland. So when the priest began to speak about "resist not evil," my ears pointed straight up, and I stared hard, taking in every word.

I didn't understand exactly what he was saying. The thing that I got most was that the more you hate something and fight it, the stronger it becomes. God created the entire world, good and bad, but until you put a name on something, it's neither good nor bad; it's just another of God's creations. Embrace something you hate as you would a friend, and it will shrivel away to nothing. Fight it, and it will feed on your hate and grow into a monster. I guess that doesn't make much sense, but that's how it came through to me. I had to reach out and put a hand on Michael's arm, and for once I didn't feel rejected when he tossed his elbow aside to dislodge it.

Afterwards we went for a drive up into the mountains toward Pecos. Then we drove back to Santa Fe in time for lunch at our favorite place just off the plaza where we ordered enchiladas made with blue corn tortillas.

When we got home that night I telephoned Philomena and told her yes, we'd be there for Papá's homecoming.

* * *

Junior was chattering the whole time we were driving to Los
Rafas that next Saturday. Michael slumped in the corner of the
back seat with his arms across his chest looking sullen.

"Be sure and tell Grandpa how good he looks," I said when
we turned west on Rafas Road toward the river.

"What if he doesn't?" Michael smart-mouthed.

I snapped my head around. "You sit up and look pleasant!" I
said. "I don't want to hear anymore from you."

A look of recognition passed between the boys. Gabe took his
right hand off the steering wheel and patted me on the leg, and I
put my angry hand on his.

By the time we turned north off Rafas Road toward Los
Griegos, I was feeling calmer. Visiting my parents always made
me jumpy. I hadn't seen Papá since the last time I had visited him
at the state hospital. The doctors said he would be all right. His
liver wasn't too damaged, and he was well dried out. But then he
had been dried out before.

We bounced along the rutted country road. I started to feel
sick to my stomach the minute I made out the old rutted drive
that went back from the road and over the irrigation ditch and
alongside the house. The trees around which the drive circled
seemed to lean back and tsk-tsk at me like a cluster of old aunties
whispering to each other about this niece of theirs who had
abandoned her Mamá.

Brown little faces popped out from among the stalks of corn
in the field and stared at the car curiously. Then all of Philomena's other grandchildren, ranging from about Michael's age
down to toddlers, emptied out of the field and surrounded the
car, waiting to size up these city cousins whom they rarely saw.

María came to the screen door to greet us. "It's about time,"
she shouted, and she lifted a water tumbler toward us in a
boozer's benediction.

I didn't bother to look at my watch. I knew it was just five-
thirty, and that was when we were supposed to be here. Gabe and
I went in, leaving Michael and Junior outside with their cousins.
Freddy smiled and lifted another glass toward us. A man we
didn't know stood and waited to be introduced.

"This is Pierre," María said. He didn't look like any Pierre to
me. With his very dark skin and black hair and eyes and his
solemn, fleshy but handsome face, he looked more like Sitting

Bull. "He's an actor. He just finished a part in—" She mentioned a popular TV western that had recently been on location here. "They wanted him to go to Hollywood, but he couldn't stand to leave New Mexico."

I half expected Pierre to grunt an "Ugh!" at us, but he said in a very nice Spanish how glad he was to meet us. He had heard a lot about us.

Then I saw *them* sitting together on the old sofa, and I went and gave Papá a hug. "Aren't you going to say hello to your old mother?" Philomena complained. I gave her a hug too. She was wrapped in a huge woolen shawl that collapsed when I put my arms around her. My hands stopped in surprise where her shoulders used to be, then went on to where they had shrunk.

She didn't even let me say anything to Papá before she was at it. "Tony sends his apologies from San Francisco. He's tied up with business and can't get away. He said he'd try to telephone long distance if he got a chance.

"And Manny," she continued, "joined the Navy and is somewhere on the high seas on a secret mission."

All I could do was stare at my shoes. I didn't dare look at anybody, although I imagine they all felt as uncomfortable about her lies as I did and were looking at their own shoes so that there was no danger of our glances meeting.

"Papá Baca," Gabe said, breaking the ice, "you look just great."

Papá smiled and lifted a glass at us. "Seven-Up," he said.

"How about it?" María asked, lifting her glass at us again.

Gabe fixed himself a highball and brought me a plain Seven-Up. We sat around while María bragged about her new boyfriend for our benefit, then extolled the virtues of family life for his benefit, with little anecdotes about close we all were and what fun we had growing up—things that never happened as far as I could remember.

Meanwhile Freddy was getting sloshed to the eyeballs. We could hear the children shouting outside as they played hide-and-seek. Philomena had closed her eyes and her mouth, and I didn't know if she was asleep or just listening until I saw this little chicken claw reach out from under the shawl to put it tighter around her.

It was unnatural being in the same room with Mamá and not

having her dominate the conversation. It was as if her fantasies about Tony and Manny had exhausted her. I sat and stared at her, occasionally looking aside to smile at Papá. I knew she couldn't walk very well anymore. Her left side was partially paralyzed from her most recent stroke. But I had no idea she would be so weak.

Finally Papá spoke in that quiet way that came from being forever overwhelmed by the talky women he lived with. "María. Don't you think it's time?"

A quick look at her watch, then María jumped to her feet and let go of her glass long enough to clap her hands. "Time to go to dinner. Everybody out to the cars."

Papá picked up Philomena like she was a rag doll. I could see that under her shawl she had on her best dress. Her eyes popped open, and her face brightened like a child anticipating a treat. "We're going dancing," she whispered. Papá nodded as he carried her through the door.

When we got outside, one of the neighbors was gathering up the smaller children to take them across the field to her house with a promise of ice cream if they ate up all their beanballs. Gabe pulled Freddy into our car to make sure he wouldn't try to drive, and the older kids piled into the back seat. We followed Pierre back to Rafas Road, west to Río Grande Boulevard, then south to Old Town.

Two waiters rearranged some tables so all twelve of us could sit together. The kids munched on tacos, and the rest of us had New Mexico style enchiladas which are the kind with the corn tortillas stacked one on top of another like pancakes and all the goodies between each layer, topped by red chili and a fried egg if you wanted one.

Papá would eat a bite, then offer a tiny morsel to Philomena who would open her little bird beak and nibble at it before she closed her eyes again. When dinner was over and we were arguing about going dancing and what to do with the children, Philomena came to life. "I want all of my family with me on this special occasion," she said. That ended that, except for a quiet "Whoopee" from one of María's daughters.

When we got to the nightclub, we left Freddy asleep in the car and trooped in. I don't know whether it was María or Pierre who knew the manager, but it was a good thing one of them did because it took a lot of persuasion before they would let us in with five children.

When we were all seated, a trio of guitarists came to our table and sang the birthday song, "Las Mañanitas," and a waiter brought over a cake with a lighted candle in the middle of it. When I looked in surprise at María, she winked at me. That was almost the last I saw of her for awhile because she and Pierre went out on the dance floor the minute the band started. María's thirteen-year old daughter dragged Michael onto the dance floor, and although he protested, he didn't rush back to the table.

"I'm so glad you're home, Papá," I said, placing my hand on his. "This is such a nice party." He smiled and nodded at Philomena whose eyes were closed again. I realized that this was the first time in a long time that we had been alone.

"Did they treat you all right in the hospital?" I asked. It seemed to me very inhumane that someone with a drinking problem would be put in the same place with people who were legally insane. I mean I didn't expect one of those wretched places you see in movies about Victorian England, but it seemed strange that if you had enough money you could be treated in a private clinic that was sort of like going to a resort for a rest, while if you were poor no one seemed to give a damn.

For the first time that evening Papá's face turned solemn. I could have bit my tongue. "Everything was white," he said. "The nurses' uniforms. The doctors' uniforms. The sheets. The walls. I got very tired of white." He looked at me with his solemn Indian face.

"My private zoo didn't like white," he said. He meant the bugs, snakes, and other such that used to crawl out of the walls at him. "And of course your Grandma Baca didn't like to visit me there. You can't see ghosts standing against a white wall. They blend right in."

That's what I get for opening my big mouth, I thought. I tried to send Gabe a thought message to ask me to dance, but Philomena started to stir. She opened her eyes and stared at me. I could tell she hadn't been asleep but had been listening to every word.

"You went to the hospital," she said, "more than you ever came home to visit me."

Gabe put a hand on my arm as if that would absorb some of the anger he knew I felt. I didn't dare say a word because I knew that whatever I said would come out wrong.

"Grandma Baca said she would see me in heaven," Papá continued, as if he hadn't heard Philomena. "Then she popped right into the white wall and never came back."

"I don't know why I ever had so much trouble with you," Philomena said, still looking at me. "I never had any trouble with my other children. I've been thinking about that a lot lately."

"Do you want to dance, Mamá?" Papá asked her.

She shook her head feebly, her eyes still fixed on me with a strange, questioning look as if she had never seen me before.

"You know what it is, Rose?" she said. "The trouble is that of all my children you're the one who turned out like me."

Hit me with a two-by-four, I thought. Then drive over me with a pickup truck while I'm flat on my back.

Papá slid his chair from the table without a word. Then he bent over Philomena and picked her up in his arms and carried her to the dance floor. All I could see were her burning, questioning eyes peering over Papá's shoulder at me. When they spun around to the music you could see her slippered feet dangling a foot above the floor as Papá held her tightly.

"She'll never change," I said to Gabe. The smaller children at the table were giggling and pointing at their grandmother. It seemed to me that everybody in the nightclub was staring at her.

"Come on, Let's dance," Gabe said.

"I don't want to dance."

"Let it go," he said. "It's Papá's party. Enjoy it for him."

I watched them on the dance floor. Then Michael and his cousin danced into view, laughing and shuffling awkwardly.

I don't believe in heredity, a voice within me said. Only to be answered by another voice that kept whispering: Resist not evil.

Papá was having a good time, smiling and nodding to the other dancers as he moved smoothly with the music, while Philomena hung dangling like a papoose carried in front instead of in back.

My God, I thought. She's not that much older than me. Fifty-five. Sixty. She'd never tell us children her age. And she looks ninety-five. What a hard life she's lived!

Gabe stood and fastened that stern macho glower at me. "Come on!" he ordered.

I was on the verge of letting him have a blast when the whisper, Resist not evil, delayed me long enough that I was on my feet and moving onto the dance floor before I could get mad. They were playing a slow rhumba, and after awhile I lost myself in the music and the motion, and everything started to get better.

We danced another couple of dances, watching Papá finally move off the floor to the table. He set Philomena down gently in her chair. Her eyes were closed, and she looked fast asleep. Then I saw Papá flag a waiter, and a moment later the waiter returned with a shot glass that he set down in front of him.

"Something's wrong," I said to Gabe as I dragged him off in the middle of the number.

Papá and Philomena were all alone. The younger children were at the edge of the dance floor staring and moving in rhythm to the music.

When we approached, Papá looked up at me with pleading in his tearful eyes. I rushed to Philomena and put my hand to her thin little chest.

"Shall I call a doctor?" Gabe asked.

I shook my head. Oh, the indignity of it happening to her here. "It's too late," I said. "Let's just carry her to the car and take her home."

Papá was starting to blubber, and I knew we were on the verge of a scene. Gabe picked up Philomena, and I took Papá by the hand as we made our way out. She looked peacefully asleep, the poor woman. Then I came back and worked my way through the dancers to tell María to round up the kids.

I made my way back across the dance floor and out to the parking lot before the full impact hit me. I started to cry. For the life of me, I didn't know if it was because Philomena was dead or because the last thing she had said to me was that I was just like her.

My knees gave as I reached the car, but Gabe caught me and hugged me and sat me down. Papá was in the back seat cradling Philomena's body while Freddy snored.

"She did the best she could," Gabe whispered to me. "That's all any of us can do."

Then the sound of the automobile starter masked Papá's whimpers, Freddy's snores, and my tears, and I reached back and took poor Mamá's hand that was already turning cold.

Celebration

Ben Montoya stared thoughtfully at the door of the compartment in the marble walled columbarium. It was slightly larger than those rare eight-inch by ten-inch photographs in the old family album that celebrated weddings and other life milestones of past generations. Chiseled into the marble door was simply: "Robert Trujillo 1914-1983," while behind, in its final resting place, was the small urn of ashes, all that remained of his once favorite uncle.

"Let us pray," the priest intoned. Ben shifted his gaze past the sign above the vase admonishing unwatered flowers only so as not to stain the marble, past the meager gathering to the gray-haired priest. The priest's teeth protruded and his mouth bulged unnaturally as he spoke with moist aspiration. "Our Father, which art in heaven . . ."

Only Uncle Bob's youngest sister Mary and Ben were related by blood to the deceased, plus, of course, Mary's children and grandchildren. All the rest were relatives of Mary's husband, Johnny.

Ben felt uncomfortable joining his voice in prayer with the chorus of mostly strangers. Almost as uncomfortable, he thought, as the spirit hovering above the remains of Bob's material body that many mistake for a person's reality. For his Uncle Bob, Roberto as he was baptized, had been a fallen away Catholic of the better kind—the kind who could be reclaimed at death by families faithful enough or charitable enough, or Ben thought, superstitious enough, to believe that final rites somehow made up for a life long drifted away from family hopes. While Ben was of the worst kind, the next younger generation who thoughtfully, willfully, earnestly abandoned the faith he was born into and that no life, no matter how well lived, could quite redeem.

He heard his non-Catholic wife beside him join in prayer, and heard too the gentle tones of relief as Aunt Mary sighed the words.

"Oh, God," Mary had whispered to Ben as they had sat in the front pew of the chapel waiting for the priest to pull his white vestments over the black trousers and black short-sleeved shirt. "Now I'll never have to worry about him again."

Her face had been pained, and she had touched his arm in silent recognition that it had only been a year since her elder sister, Ben's mother, had passed away.

The service in the small chapel had been short. What had Father Noonan called it? A prayer gathering? What remained of Ben's Catholic knowledge was thirty years out of date: pre-meat on Friday, pre-English Mass, with a vague impression that cremation was at least frowned upon if not actually disallowed. Was this why a prayer gathering and not a Mass? Or had the priest known about the circumstances of Bob's death, or more disturbing, the circumstances of his life?

"At least," Mary had continued, "he will never be alone again. He'll be with God." For Bob, the "baby," had been the only one of that large family who had never married, had never spawned his replacements in profusion as had his several brothers and sisters.

Ben had looked away uneasily. Beneath her words lay the unspoken reality. For Bob had made a choice. Or rather, had assiduously avoided the responsibility of commitment. He was of a generation when bachelorhood did not conjure up suspicions of sexual deviancy, for in truth there had been girl friends over the years—but no commitment.

No. What choice had been made in his life was his liver's self-indulgent pursuit of self-destruction. For the last time Ben had *not* seen Bob had been at Ben's mother's funeral. He was not feeling well, Bob had whined over the telephone. He was under a doctor's care. And he truly might have been, for his trembling voice might just as easily have been illness as alcohol.

His death had been sudden, although it had been expected any moment for years. Only Ben's youngest sister still lived in Los Angeles where Bob had died. The rest of the family had either moved back to New Mexico or north to the San Francisco Bay area. So it had been Ben's sister who had received the printed form postcard to contact the Police Department about the remains of (written in the blank space by hand) Robert Trujillo.

"He'd been dead over a week," she had telephoned Ben. "The ID card in his wallet listed mother and me as nearest of kin." Then she began to cry, not for Bob but for their mother. When she calmed down she said, "Why didn't they contact me right away? My phone number was in his wallet. Those damned police!"

Then, of course, the grisly details. The crowded morgue, wall-to-wall with hunks of dead meat, not like the neat, sterile drawers in the movies or on television. The nose broken, misshapen, hanging sideways on his face. The bruised cheek and blue-black left eye. The thin, bony remains with skin like dry parchment, as if all the juices had evaporated at the moment of death. She signed for his personal effects, and a clerk brought out a small envelope containing the scuffed wallet empty of cash, a book of matches, a soiled handkerchief, a comb with fewer teeth than the dead man, a ballpoint pen with Federal Savings & Loan imprinted along the barrel, and thirty-eight cents in change.

Her first thought, she said, and it had been Ben's thought too as he listened to her, was that he had been attacked and robbed. "They found him on the bathroom floor of his room," she said. Her voice was tinged with distaste, as if tiptoeing around the words. Ben knew the hotel where Bob had lived, one of those decaying relics in what was left of the downtown slum, inhabited by transient winos, illegal aliens, the unemployed who still had the price of a room, and other down-and-outers, most still on their way down.

He had driven his uncle there a few times when his mother had been alive and Bob had taken the bus to the suburbs for a family holiday gathering. He had never said anything to his uncle about the place, only nodding when a shamefaced, sober Bob had spoken of its convenience and closeness to work. The last time Bob had repeated this apologetic explanation he had been retired from the post office for over three years.

His sister went on, the words slower now as if she was distracted and thinking of something else. "It looked like he had the DT's and took a nasty fall, but it was probably cirrhosis that killed him." Then she began to cry—she must have been thinking about their mother again. "I phoned Aunt Mary," she finally said. "She and Johnny are coming down next week to fill out the papers and go through his room. She wants to ship the body up north if they can afford it. Nobody from Albuquerque wants anything to do with it."

Minutes later there was a telephone call from Mary to repeat what Ben's sister had already told him. Then, after her return from Los Angeles, another call, teary this time, reminiscing. "Bob had been such a handsome man. He was always so neat about his clothes. Oh, God, it broke my heart to see him like that."

Then she complained bitterly that when she had telephoned the hotel, the manager had not wanted to let her into his room, relenting only when she had threatened to call the police. When they arrived, he had grumbled as if doing them a special favor. When he unlocked the door and let them in, Mary knew why.

The room was neat, the way she remembered Bob. But it was not so much neat from care as it was from lack of anything that could create clutter. There were a few simple kitchen utensils, including breakfast dishes in the sink, and the evening newspaper from the day before he died on the kitchen table. His clothes closet was empty except for a few well-worn shirts, two old pairs of trousers, some neckties, a jacket, and a worn out pair of shoes. She sensed that it had been burglarized of worthwhile clothing and was immediately suspicious of the manager.

The lock on the other closet where he kept his valuables was broken. His cameras were missing, and the only item of value was a photographic enlarger that was too heavy to be easily carried away.

"I was so angry!" Mary said. "I wanted to call the police right then! But I didn't know what was left when he died. God, he might have pawned those things or given them away. His bank statement showed that he had recently written checks for large amounts for who knows what. Maybe the Mexican lady down the hall who used to cook for him once in awhile. There isn't enough money left to ship him up here and bury him."

Thus it was, against all her instincts, that Mary relented and let the L.A. County crematory do its job. It was Ben's sister who, after the several days wait for a turn in the furnace and a legal release, shipped the ashes north.

"It was such a little box," his sister had said on the telephone. "That's all there is left of him."

Father Noonan closed his missal and made the sign of the cross. "Name of the Father . . . Son . . . Holy Ghost."

"Amen," the crowd answered.

Then he turned and placed the missal on the waist-high marble block behind him and took up a gold vessel with the handle of a holy water sprinkler protruding above the lip. He nodded at Aunt Mary, then set off in solemn procession deeper into the mausoleum where the urn was stored. The crowd rose and followed to the marble wall for the rest of the service.

"Robert Trujillo 1914-1983." But Ben was thinking about 1938, for that was his earliest recollection of Bob. He didn't want to think of that sick old man who had drunk himself to death. Or of the times over the years before he moved up north that he had helped his mother put Bob in the hospital. Even the state hospital for the mentally ill in Camarillo once. No, he wanted to remember the late 1930's, the Great Depression, when Bob first took the bus from Albuquerque to Los Angeles to look for work.

Ben's parents had rented that little frame house on 47th Street, the one with the double garage, half of which served as Bob's apartment that first summer. Ben had been in the third grade and have never lived near a young uncle before. One who would come walking jauntily down the street, whistling the tune whose words Ben and his sister knew from listening to the radio.

"Lookie, lookie, lookie . . . here comes cookie . . . walking down the street."

"Cookie!" they would scream as if that was his name, and run to search his pockets for chewing gum.

Later that summer his parents had sent them to their room while they talked behind closed doors with Bob. Ben had pressed an ear against the wall and tried to listen, but all he heard was a few angry words about streetcar fare and going to the follies downtown instead of looking for a job. Very shortly after, their uncle started washing dishes in a restaurant—he was a pearl diver he jokingly told them—and moved out.

But what Ben would never forget as long as he lived was his tenth birthday. Times had been hard, the boy knew. Only a few days before, his mother had found a five-dollar bill in the gutter, and for awhile Ben knew he was going to get something wonderful for his birthday. But then his parents had a family council, and he remembered overhearing the low voices in the next room saying that his father would get a new pair of shoes this time because he had to go to work, while Mother would do without until things got better.

Ben had blinked his eyes and tightened his lips. There would be no something wonderful, not even a party. Although Mother might bake a cake and maybe make ice cream if the ice cream freezer was working. Cheap, homemade ice cream. Vanilla.

He and his sister sat solemnly on the front steps the late afternoon of his birthday. Sure, there would be ice cream and cake after dinner, but that wasn't a real birthday. Not like the one Buddy Goff down the street had last month.

They were so downcast that they did not look toward the merrily whistled tune. "Lookie, lookie, lookie . . . here comes cookie . . ." Their forearms hung dejectedly between parted knees. Only when footsteps approached, accompanied by the whirring sound of rubber on cement, did his sister look up.

"Ben!" she shouted. "Look!"

Coming up the walk, his hands holding lightly onto the handle bars, was their Uncle Bob. Ben's heart pounded so hard that he thought he was going to faint.

"Cookie!" he screamed.

His uncle stopped in front of the house, a grin on his face, his eyes sparkling. "I walked it all the way," he said. "Since it's your birthday, you have to be the first to ride it."

With a whoop he ran to the two-wheeler, so excited that he was incoherent. "A bike!" he shouted. "A bike! A bike!"

He didn't notice that it was used, although freshly painted. He didn't notice his uncle's pleased smile, nor realize then that his uncle had never in his life owned a bicycle. He leaped onto the seat, and steadied by Bob's firm hands, pedaled down the sidewalk to the end of the block and back.

"Oh, Uncle Bob!" he shouted. "This is the most wonderful birthday I've ever had!"

And it was. For of all the more than forty birthdays since, none approached it. And of all the celebrations since, only that Christmas when their first child had been four years old, old enough to know a little of what Christmas meant, had exceeded it. It hadn't been the gifts: the bicycle on Ben's tenth birthday, or the cowboy boots from Grandpa and the little train from Santa Claus for their oldest son. Those had just been material things like the urn of ashes in the compartment behind the marble door. It had been the love that had been behind the giving, that powerful invisible caring that even the youngest could feel.

Father Noonan whispered to a teenage boy, one of Aunt Mary's many grandsons, who stepped beside the priest and took the gold vessel from him. The priest's voice was low as he addressed the group. "If you would all take turns and sprinkle holy water on the compartment." He turned, whispering words only he could hear, and gave three shakes with the sprinkler. Then he silently handed the sprinkler to Aunt Mary, who sprinkled the door of the chamber, then passed it on to her husband who did his duty, then handed it to Ben. As he stepped closer to the wall, he saw the pale stain on the chest of the priest's white vestment, then above it the soft, friendly eyes.

The sprinkler passed through the crowd, even to the tiny hands of tots whose fists were guided by their mothers. The priest said a final prayer, then announced that the service was over.

Ben stepped back from the crowd and looked up and down and along the marble walls of the columbarium. He read the names, many of them Slavic, farmers who had first settled this now urban area. Many of them Spanish, like his Uncle Bob's.

"You're coming to the house, aren't you?" his Aunt Mary whispered.

He nodded automatically, his thoughts far away. It would be so easy to send a check to the church and have a Mass said for Bob. So easy and so impersonal, like so much that passed for life these days.

Ben looked over the three generations in the crowd, his eyes resting longest on the youngsters. Most children had bicycles these days. Many of them had those oversize portable radios that assault you on the street. And some even had video games. He realized that he didn't even know any poor children anymore. Life had been good to him that way.

He took a final look at the words carved in marble: "Robert Trujillo 1914-1983" and heard the spritely whistle that no one else heard. "Lookie, lookie, lookie . . . here comes . . ." He knew he would have to give a bicycle to a poor child somewhere, maybe in one of those children's homes. For that was something Uncle Bob would enjoy more than another Mass, maybe even more than one final toast before downing one final shot of whiskey. At least Ben would like to think so.

Tío Ignacio's Stigmata

Tía Sophie Gutiérrez wrote Mamá that Tío Ignacio was deathly ill. Since Sophie is a living, breathing tragedy queen—someday they'll do her life on a TV soap opera—Mamá did not know what to do. She knew that a telephone call would be a waste of breath, and she did not want to spend the bus fare from Tucson to San José if it was another of Sophie's "dramas." Yet Ignacio was her oldest brother, and she worried about him. So she wrote to me since I was already in California teaching at Southwestern U.

"Damn it!" I said, waving the letter at my wife, Lola. "I've been looking forward to this Easter vacation like no other in my life. I need a rest from people."

"This is familia," Lola said.

"Sophie is not related to me by blood," I said. "And she's a pain in the ass."

"¡Emiliano Zapata Rosca! ¡Familia!"

You think Anglo liberals are burdened with guilt. Just whip a Chicano with the words "familia" and a thunderbolt shatters his soul like the first fall from grace in the Garden of Eden. Especially if the whip is in the hands of a woman like Lola who can lay a more powerful guilt trip than the most Jewish of Jewish mothers.

So I changed the oil and adjusted the points of my tired old Chevy—we used to pronounce it Tschevy in the barrio—and got ready to head north toward San José. "Two days," I told Lola. "I'll be back on Good Friday so we can go to St. Pancho's for the stations of the cross."

"Just be sure you're back Sunday to give Junior and Lolita their Easter baskets." Such faith that woman.

From the environs of Southwestern U where we live, it's a

straight shot north on Highway 5. The old Tschevy climbed past
Gorman and Lebec to Wheeler Ridge as I watched for big trucks
and the Highway Patrol. The twitching radiator needle dropped
as the car descended to the valley near Bakersfield.

There's not much to see on Highway 5 in contrast to the old
highway. Old Highway 99 went through all the towns that grow
the crops that give so many Chicanos stooped shoulders, bent
backs, arthritic legs, and wrinkles and gray hair before their
time. Towns like Delano. And Tulare. Visalia. Fresno. Madera.
Chowchilla. A litany of stoop labor and hot sun and the drudg-
ery of survival.

Luckily it's reasonably cool through the valley in April. The
110-degree days come later. And I made my way quickly to the
turn-off to Gilroy and Highway 101 that led to San José. Five and
a half hours tops since the Tschevy was behaving.

I only got lost once trying to find Tío Ignacio's and Tía
Sophie's house. It's in an old part of the city—it's grown too
much to be called a town anymore—a block from some railroad
tracks and not far from an old cemetary where the weeds are
fighting the old stone markers for possession; the weeds have
already strangled the dried wooden crosses.

San José reminds me a lot of parts of L.A. Hot. Dry. Flat.
With funny little flat-roofed houses and only a few trees, although there's an occasional palm.

What lawn there was in their front yard was sparse and dry,
like a bald man's head with scraggly tufts of hair here and there.
But the plum tree was vigorous and showed signs of bearing
fruit. The little piece of paper tacked over the doorbell said "Out
of Order," so I knocked.

I heard the sound of footsteps; then the door opened slowly,
just wide enough for a suspicious dark eye to glare out at me.

"It's me, Tía. Your nephew, Emiliano Rosca."

The door opened wider, but she still had that suspicious look
on her face, now subtly tinged with pain. "He's dying," she said
in a quavering voice. "If you had come tomorrow it would have
been too late." Then almost as if on cue, a tear rolled down her
left cheek.

I hadn't visited my aunt and uncle since I finished graduate
school, which was a few years ago, but their place looked the
same. It was paint-chipped clapboard outside, and as I stepped

into the sala ("living room" as you say in Anglo), it was like going back in time. The same linoleum was on the floor, spotlessly cleaned and waxed but even more faded. There were those cloth doodads on the arms and back of Tío Ignacio's stuffed chair. On the wall to the right of the built-in electric heater was the picture gallery. At the center was a sad-faced Jesus pointing his fingers to the flaming red heart that always reminded me of an over-grown avocado seed. Surrounding it was the family triad of modern saints: a smiling JFK with wind-tossed hair; his grim-faced brother, Robert; and one of our own, a kind-faced but solemn looking César Chávez. Beyond these photos was a wall full of familia. Their five children, numerous grandchildren, brothers, sisters, nieces, nephews including me in my college cap and gown—on and on and on.

"Your Mamá didn't come," Sophie said. There was accusation in her voice.

My mind raced for an excuse. Then, catching myself in this old pattern, I thought: Stop it, Emiliano! Don't get trapped into playing her game.

A dark-faced little girl peeked around the corner of the door to the kitchen, one of the grandchildren no doubt. I was certain that all of her children had fled home as soon as they were old enough or even sooner, moving as far from Mamá as they could. At the sight of the little girl my blood surged with triumph, and I could not help but consider giving Tía Sophie tit for tat. Her grandchildren would not be here unless one of Sophie's children was in desperate trouble.

"How's the family?" I asked, trying hard not to let what I was thinking show through. "Everybody all right?"

She threw me a look that would have frozen a lesser man. I could see the struggle on her face, hear it like the silent voice of anger she must have felt: Should she lie? Should she tell me the truth about how bad it really was? Was it any of my business?

She didn't answer. Her head turned quick as lightning toward her granddaughter. "Go outside and play!" she snapped. But this was not a prelude to a confession meant only for adult ears. Instead she led me to the side bedroom where, lights out and shades drawn, I could see the thin little stick of a shape under the covers. "What am I going to do?" she whispered. "It's a terrible thing to happen to a poor old lady." Then she was

gone, and I stood a moment waiting for my eyes to adjust to the
dim light in that warm, stuffy little room,

I went over and sat on the chrome and plastic kitchen chair
beside the bed. It was like vigils I remembered over old and
dying members of the family, especially Grandfather Rosca's
final days when I was a boy.

Tío Ignacio's eyes were closed, and he breathed with a low
growl that was like the peaceful snore of a child. The light
blanket was tucked under his armpits, and his arms were
stretched out to the sides, hands wrapped in white gauze. I
wondered what fatal illness attacked his hands. Leprosy? Elec-
trocution by grabbing a live power line?

"He has already been sick over a week, and if he doesn't go
back to work next week we'll probably have to go on welfare. It's a
disgrace."

I hadn't even heard Tía Sophie re-enter. I turned toward the
whispering voice, but she had left as quickly as she had come. All
that remained was a trembling of air like the aftermath of a
visitation from another world.

"Mierda," I heard a deep, hoarse voice whisper.

I turned back in surprise. The thin little body was still tucked
under the blanket, but Tío Ignacio's right eye was open. "The
way she carries on," he said, "you'd think it was she who was
chosen, not me."

Chosen? I thought. Some choosing.

As if in answer, he raised his arms out to the side and let them
drop onto the mattress. Was it a sign of hopelessness? Or did it
have some other significance?

"How are you, nephew? How's your Mamá?" I nodded that
she was fine as he popped open his other eye and turned his face
toward me. "Did she tell you?"

I didn't know if he meant Tía Sophie or my mother. "Only
that you've been sick."

With his bandaged hands he pulled on the blanket until it
popped out of the corners at the foot of the bed, then up and
over his ankles. Like his hands, his feet were wrapped in white
gauze discolored by what must have been pale dried blood. Then
he folded down the top of the blanket to his waist and raised his
pajama shirt. His body just below his breast was also wrapped.

"The five wounds of Christ," he said. "I've been chosen." He made a sign of the cross with his bandaged right hand, and his face glowed with satisfaction.

I didn't know what to say. I'm of a different generation from mi tío, and my Catholicism is not so deeply rooted. I guess what I'm trying to say is that I don't believe in miracles, and here was one being presented to me—I think.

But I didn't have to ask how it happened. He was watching me warily, and when I didn't respond right away he spoke again in that deep manly voice that, as a boy, I always marvelled at coming from such a small man. It was as if inside there was a giant trying to get free.

"The stigmata," he said, "they appeared one morning about a week ago. Though God didn't speak to me, I knew that I had been chosen. It's a sign of all the suffering in my life. El dolor de la raza. A sign that God knows and has me on His list."

"Sure, Tío."

"And all that stuff about welfare—you know Sophie. If God gave her a million dollar bill, she'd complain because the bill was too new and looked fake. I've been the janitor at the elementary school for years. I only missed two days work so far; this week is a holiday. But Sophie—" He shook his head slowly from side to side.

I felt uncomfortable about how to ask the question that was itching inside of me: How dangerous was it? Except for those bandages he didn't look any worse than he had ever looked over the years.

"What—did the doctor say?"

A strange expression crossed his face. He looked at me with what I thought were frightened, pleading eyes. Had the doctor told him something he could not tell anyone else?

"I need peace and quiet," he said. "Lots of rest. After that it's up to God."

But I felt uncomfortable at his explanation. The words did not sound sincere. He was hiding something.

I sat quietly watching him for a moment. The lines on his forehead seemed to shift like subtle, slow waves, and his eyes were lost in thought. When he looked at me again, it was as if he was considering whether or not to tell me. I had always been one of his favorites, mainly because I was the only one in the family who had gone to college, and he had as much respect for an

educated man as he had for a priest. He had not been so lucky
with his own sons. He was just grateful that they had managed to
stay out of jail.

But the moment passed, and he did not speak. "You're tired,
Tío," I said. "I'd better leave you now."

He nodded and grasped my hand. "Come back later," he
said. "We'll talk some more." Then his lids flickered, and when I
looked back from the door his eyes were closed.

Back in the sala all was a quiet whirlwind. Tía Sophie had
repolished the already spotless floor. The furniture had been
shifted around so she could get behind the pieces.

She was busy dusting the photo gallery and spoke at me
without missing a stroke. "The reporters from the paper will be
here tomorrow. There might even be TV."

My mouth dropped open in astonishment. "Not the Mer-
cury-News," she said. "The other one." She mentioned the
name. The Barrio Blab, I called it. Gang wars. Gossip. Witches.
All in Spanish and not very good Spanish at that.

"I don't believe it."

She stopped mid-stroke and frowned at me. "How often does
a woman have a husband who wakes up with the wounds of
Christ? Just before Easter, too. They want to interview me." She
puffed up like a bird preening its feathers.

I made my way to the screened back porch which was for
guests and threw myself onto the narrow bed. It felt like a coffin
when I hit the hard suface. The window was open, and I could
hear the kids playing outside.

How does a man stay married for forty years to a woman like
Sophie? I thought. There he was in bed, the poor wretch, while
she was getting ready to talk to reporters and go on TV. If
there's any justice, God should have hurled a thunderbolt at her
instead of giving those silly wounds to Tío Ignacio.

I lay on my back staring at the ceiling, drifting into a relaxed
drowsiness when I heard a rattle at the screen door. The granddaughter's face was pressed against the wire staring at me.

"Why do they call you Pata?" she asked.

"I was named for Emiliano Zapata. Pata is short for Zapata."

Her eyes shifted slyly. "Grandma says pata means foot, and
you usually put it in your mouth." She giggled and ran off to join
her gangster playmates.

I turned my gaze back up, and it wasn't long before I was dead asleep. I'm not sure how long I slept before I heard the voices. It was dark outside so it could have been ten at night or four in the morning.

"They're my wounds!" The basso profundo echoed throughout the small house. "And I don't want no reporters or no TV! The only ones I'll talk to are the priest, the Bishop, or the Pope!"

"You're ruining my life!" Tía Sophie screamed back. "My one big chance!"

Then a door slammed abruptly, and the house was deathly still. For a moment I was tempted to tiptoe to my uncle and make sure he was all right. The last thing a sick man needs is a quarrel with his wife. But a few moments of staring at the darkness dispelled the idea. Instead I slipped out of my clothes and under the blanket. That was all I remember until the smell of bacon woke me.

"You didn't eat dinner last night," Tía Sophie nagged. The implication was that not eating was a personal affront to her hospitality and her cooking, and would result in sickliness, disease, and invalidism, adding to her already considerable burdens.

"Smells good," I said hungrily, not taking the bait.

She served a plate of two fried eggs, bacon, and thin little slices of fried potato mixed with green chili, plus a side order of flour tortillas. After she poured two cups of coffee, she sat across the table from me. "I need to talk to you, Pata," she said.

I ignored the urgency in her voice because I was too intent on breakfast.

"You're a college man. You can tell me. What I want to know is: Should I give the reporters a free sample of holy water?"

I forgot the good manners my Mamá taught me and spoke with my mouth full. "Holy water?"

"Well. Not really holy. It hasn't been blessed yet. It's the water from the kitchen tap Ignacio drinks from. It must be miraculous like Lourdes. Didn't you see his wounds?"

I shook my head incredulously. Although I was at a loss for words, Tía Sophie wasn't. "If he would let me change his bandages, I could cut them up into little squares and make a killing selling them. Only he won't let me. He keeps wearing the same dirty gauze he put on the first day."

I shuddered, wondering if she had considered taking a pint of blood from him to further her commercial endeavors.

"So tell me. Should I give the reporters free holy water?"

"Why not?" I said, swallowing hard whatever it was that the miracle of avarice had transformed into a cold lump. "Maybe you could snip a few threads from the True Bandage for them too."

Sophie smiled and patted my hand. Irony and she were not speaking acquaintances. I did not get a chance to remind her that Tío Ignacio did not want reporters or TV before she was gone—back to the bottling plant I suspect. Then a quiet, insistent knock on the door gave me an excuse to abandon the remains of breakfast.

A fat little woman dressed all in black, head covered by a rebozo, looked up at me with wondrous eyes and whispered as solemnly as if she were in church. "What time will the TV be here?"

Oh my God, our Lady of Channel 36, I thought. "I don't know, Señora. I suggest you wait until you see the trucks out front." She smiled and nodded before slowly descending the steps and making her way down the block.

It was like that the rest of the morning, and I finally had to leave. I drove over to the State University campus in case an old acquaintance or two might be around. If nothing else, the coffee shop might be open, and I could sit around overcaffeinating my already agitated corpuscles.

When I came back just before dinner, Tía Sophie was slumped on the easy chair in the sala accompanied by three of her black-garbed cronies. They didn't even look at me, so I knew that whatever it was had been really bad. There was an undisturbed line of little bottles with neat labels on the table. It didn't look as if a single one had been sold or given away.

"They didn't come," Sophie finally said in a sepulchral voice. "And tomorrow's Good Friday."

I didn't know what that had to do with anything, unless she had planned on Tío Ignacio dying Friday mid-afternoon. In alarm, I nodded at the ladies and hurried to the bedroom.

"Tío," I whispered. "Are you all right?"

The thin stick of a figure rolled over and faced me. "I don't want the reporters and the TV," he said. "What's that woman trying to do, kill me?"

"They didn't come," I said.

"They're waiting for tomorrow."

"You don't know that."

He turned his soulful eyes up and flashed me a look that said that any fool should know what was obvious. "She's turning me into a pimp for God," he said. "Next thing you know she'll be on those commercials on TV—the ones that sell records of the twenty greatest salsa hits or those kitchen gadgets that do everything but wash dishes for a dollar ninety-eight. She'll be selling holy water or some other blasphemous relic.

"They aren't even her wounds," he went on. "She has to grab everybody else's headache and make it her own so she can complain to the world about it."

"Why have you put up with her all these years, Tío? You could have gotten rid of her long ago?"

He looked at me in shock. "What are you saying? Divorce? That's against the Church. No," he said, shaking his head. "I'll strangle her first."

The telephone in the other room broke the silence. I turned, listening to Tía Sophie's excited voice. "You're coming tomorrow instead? You want to interview him and take some pictures? What's that? Yes, of course. I'll see that he's rested so he can talk. And I can give you all the details first since he will be too weak to talk for long. Tomorrow. Yes. Yes. Ten o'clock."

Before the receiver had clicked, Tío Ignacio was shaking his head. "Never," he said. "Over my dead body." Then he gave me that frightened, soulful look that he had given me yesterday. The one that made me so uncomfortable.

"Is everything OK, Tío?"

He turned his head to the wall and did not respond. I didn't want to be around Tía Sophie and her clums, so I rushed through the sala and out to my car to go to McDonald's for dinner. Christ, I thought. I better be around tomorrow morning to help poor old uncle. She'll drive him to the grave.

The next morning Tía Sophie insisted on cooking breakfast for me although I would have settled for an Egg McMuffin. Again she poured two cups of coffee and sat at the table.

"I want to talk to you about your uncle," she said. "I need your help."

"What did the doctor say? How serious is it? I should call up Mamá and let her know how her brother is." Although this was the third day I had been here, it was amazing that I had not yet learned anything definite about Tío's state of health beyond Tía Sophie's greeting when I first crossed the threshold. After that dramatic declaration, the matter was promptly dropped.

"The doctor," I repeated. "What does the doctor say?"

"There hasn't been any doctor."

"What?"

"I didn't send for the doctor because I was afraid he'd tell us it was something serious."

I was dumbfounded. I couldn't believe it. Sophie stared at my silent, open mouth. "You know how doctors are," she said. "Besides, I don't want to talk about doctors. I want to talk about your uncle. That stubborn mule. I don't know what's come over him. The reporters are coming at ten o'clock, and he refuses to talk to them."

So I was supposed to change Tío Ignacio's mind, I thought. Only I completely agreed with him. Whatever his affliction, it was between him and God. Or at any rate him and his parish priest or the doctor.

"I don't see how I can help, auntie."

Her look said that that was what she expected of an ingrate. For a moment I thought she was going to snatch the plate of half-eaten food and nearly full cup of coffee from me and empty them in the sink.

"All I want is a few words from him," she insisted. "I'll do all the real talking. Maybe they'll even take my picture. They definitely want a picture of Ignacio's wounds."

I hurriedly gulped the rest of my breakfast—I was hungry—and stared at her while chewing furiously. She took my silence for acquiescence.

"What I want you to do," she said, "is go into the bedroom just before ten o'clock and make sure he's awake. Get him to talk to you a little so he'll be ready. Only don't tell him about the reporters. When we come in, he'll have to say something. You stand by to help fold back the blanket to show his wounds."

"For God's sakes, auntie, the poor man wants to be left alone."

If I had been one of her children she would have reached across the table and slapped me. As it was, she couldn't decide between a fierce scowl or a poor-pitiful-little-me expression.

"This is our chance," she said. Her voice was tinged with disgust at my stupidity. "They may even put *your* picture in the paper. I telephoned the TV station, too."

I could see it all now. The TV newsbreak with the affirmative action reporter—a woman, either black, brown, or yellow—announcing in a breathless, sincere way: "San José stigmata in living color at ten o'clock. Stay tuned."

Again I didn't respond, and again Tía Sophie believed what she wanted to. What could I say? She wouldn't accept my no, so there was no point wasting my breath. The only problem was: What could I do to help poor Tío Ignacio?

When the first of the many knockings on the door began, I escaped from the kitchen to the bedroom. I think every neighbor within six blocks must have come to find out what was happening.

"The vultures are starting to gather so they can pick my bones," I heard from deep under the blanket. "They think it will turn them into peacocks that the world will notice. As if that makes any difference."

"You're awake, uncle."

The answer was a deep sigh. Then he turned and looked at me as I sat beside him. "I guess the reporters from the Mexican Inquirer are coming soon." That's what he called what I referred to as the Barrio Blab. I liked his name for it better.

As I watched him there, helpless to turn aside the onrushing tide of public hoopla, I realized how alone he was. Only one little granddaughter who could not help him. While his wife, as always, swept on like a force of nature, aware only of her own desires. It must have always been like that with Tío Ignacio. Of all of the family, only he was unable to run from the tidal wave that tried to engulf them all. And now only he remained to be battered by this whirl of mindless energy.

"What can I do to help, Tío?"

A look of gratitude flickered across his dark, wrinkled face,

and his mouth slid into a wry smile. "When this happened," he
said, nodding at his gauze-wrapped hands, "I thought it would
be something all my own. Something she couldn't try to take
over. I thought it would give me a few days rest, a few days alone.
Well—you see what's happened."

He turned and looked me full in the face, his smile still
lingering. "Thank you, nephew. There's nothing that you need
to do. It's all in God's hands. He has been my salvation all these
years." His eyes seemed to focus inward for a moment, and then
they came back to the outer world. "Yes, Pata. There is something. When those hyenas from the Mexican Inquirer come, I
want you to be here. I'll want you to help me show them. To do
what I ask you when the time comes. And to tell them that I've
been an honest man all my life and that I'm telling the truth. No
matter what anyone says, I want you to tell them that."

"Of course, uncle." But I was a little uneasy because, as I've
said before, I didn't believe in miracles even if Tío did.

"Now I'm going to take a little rest before they come." He
closed his eyes, and I stayed beside him.

It wasn't long before there was another knock on the front
door. The voice was a man's this time, speaking rapidly in a
textbook Spanish that contrasted greatly with the butchered
slang you usually hear in the barrio. It was like a very cultured
Englishman speaking with an American from Brooklyn. He was
the religious editor of the Mexican Inquirer, he said. And Ms
Archuleta was the photographer. I guess there isn't a word in
Spanish for Ms—at least I don't know one—so he said it in
English.

Then Tía Sophie went into her act. God. You could have tape
recorded it and played it verbatim on "All My Children."

The popping flashbulbs must have awakened my uncle. "Remember what I told you," he whispered. "I've been an honest
man all my life."

A moment later footsteps approached from the sala. A flashbulb almost blinded me. I could hear the cultured voice from
somewhere in the white shining aura say, "So this is the Afflicted
One?" When I recovered my sight the two of them were standing
beside the bed with Tía Sophie between them smiling proudly.

"Show them your wounds, Ignacio," she said.

"Show them, Emiliano," my uncle said.

I felt like a headwaiter ready to lift the lid off a silver platter to present a gourmet dish to starving, salivating cannibals. First I untucked the blanket from the foot of the bed, folding it neatly just below Tío Ignacio's knees. Then I folded down the top of the blanket to about his waist while he pulled his pajama top up to his chest. There, in all their glory, were the five gauze-wrapped wounds: feet, hands, and abdomen.

The flashbulbs popped in rapid succession. "Señor Gutiérrez," the editor said. "Can you tell us how this happened?"

A little smile played around the edges of Tío's mouth. "I'm just a poor, humble janitor down at the Lacey Elementary School," he said. "Not even a sanitary engineer like some fancy broom pushers call themselves."

I could see the religious editor looking around the bed with a puzzled frown, trying to see who was in there with him. Ms Archuleta stood with camera poised, also confused by Tío's booming voice.

Tío spread his arms out wide to show his hands. "This happened a week ago last Wednesday," he went on. "First the hands. Then the feet. Then my side. I was at work, cleaning up the multi-purpose room. There had been a play the night before."

"Was it a simultaneous spontaneous generation?" the editor asked. A flashbulb punctuated his question.

Tío blinked and looked up at me. "They happened one at a time. First the hands, then the feet, and last the side. The whole thing took about five minutes."

"Sequential," the editor said. "Very unusual."

"Emiliano." I nodded, thinking uncle was ready for me to cover him up again. "Would you help me take off the bandages." Ms Archuleta leaned forward, camera ready. "The hands first. Then I can do the rest."

As I carefully unwound the gauze, Tío continued to talk. "I was taking down the stage set when these happened." He held his hands palm out in front of his face. "There were some nails sticking out where I grabbed the wooden frame."

By now his left hand was unbandaged. Except for the light stains on the gauze, you could hardly see a trace of the puncture. "Mercurochrome," he said, holding up the bandage. "And a few drops of blood." Then to me as I worked on the other hand, "Just pull it off. It won't hurt."

Tía Sophie's face had clouded, and I could see the reporters giving her a steely-eyed once over. Pointing to his feet, he went on. "I wrapped my handkerchief around one hand, then started to push the wooden frame across the stage. If there had been someone to help me, it wouldn't have fallen over. But it did. The damned nails went through the tongues of my shoes into the tops of my feet." By this time those bandages were off.

Ms Archuleta had lowered her camera and turned toward her companion. Tía Sophie stepped almost nose to nose with the editor. "He's lying!" she said. "He's saying that to spite me!" Then she spun around and thrust her face at Tío. "¡Desgraciado!" Her closed fist trembled in restraint.

Tío talked on cooly as ever. "When I finally got the set put away, I accidently stuck myself in the side. It was all an accident."

The religious editor's words came out slower and even more precisely. "These . . . were . . . not . . . wounds . . . from . . . heaven?" Meanwhile the photographer had bent over Tío's feet, poking at one with a polished red fingernail.

"I came home and bandaged myself. Sophie was out. Then I thought: What a nice way to spend a few days in bed."

"Liar!" Sophie screamed.

"Tío is an honest man, and he's telling the truth," I said.

"You're the one who first talked about stigmata," Tío said to Sophie. "I didn't have the heart to disillusion you."

"Liar!" She swung an open palm and smacked him across the face.

Ms Archuleta took a last close-up of Tío's unbandaged side, then followed the editor out. They placed two bottles of complimentary clear liquid on the table as they hurried to the door.

Tía Sophie ran after them. "Wait! Wait! There's been some mistake!"

When I looked out the window I could see the TV truck pull up and the reporters saying something to the crew while Tía Sophie raised her arms and, no doubt, her voice. The crew got back into the truck and drove off behind the reporters from the Mexican Inquirer.

"I'd better stay here with you, Tío," I said. "God knows what Aunt Sophie will do. She's madder than hell."

"Serves her right for jumping to conclusions. My only sin was letting it go this far so I could get a few days peace and quiet.

And nephew, I have to apologize for not telling you the truth at the very first. Once this thing got started, it took on a life of its own."

I stayed with Tío the rest of that day, after telephoning my wife that I wouldn't make it for the stations of the cross. I had my own cross to bear—to make sure Tía Sophie cooled off before I left. Who wants a family murder on his conscience?

We didn't see Tía Sophie the rest of that afternoon, so I fixed dinner for Tío and me. Afterwards, as I was washing the dishes, there was a timid knock on the door. The round little neighbor lady dressed in black smiled at me when I answered. "Sophie made the afternoon papers," she said, holding up the Mexican Inquirer so I could read the front page. I'm sure it was Tío's paper she had picked up from the steps, but I guess the dear lady didn't want us to miss it.

"San José Stigmata Hoax!" screamed the headline. Just beneath it was a photograph of Tío's gauze-wrapped extremities alongside another photograph of a sour looking Tía Sophie. The lurid details were below.

"There wasn't any TV?" the neighbor asked sweetly.

No, I shook my head as I shut the door. I peeked out the curtains apprehensively, searching for Mike Wallace and a cameraman. I could see it all on "60 Minutes"—"Religious Relic Swindle in California," and a finger pointing Wallace saying, "You mean you deliberately lied about a sacred thing like that—and on Good Friday?"

Tía Sophie sneaked in crestfallen a little later, and things were calm enough after that that I went back home on Saturday. Then on Easter Sunday I received a long distance phone call from San José. For the first time in her life Tía Sophie had missed Sunday Mass, and she was doomed because of this mortal sin. On Easter of all Sundays. She couldn't face all the people who had read the Mexican Inquirer, Tío said. When he had told her to shut up her blubbering and fix lunch, she had done just that. Things were going to be different from now on, he said. And by the way, happy Easter.

If he had been a cruel man, I would have felt sorry for Tía Sophie. but as it was—well—men can be liberated too. And a good confession could still save Sophie's soul. That and a better temper. Amen.

Liberation

I knew I was getting old when, in my dreams, the partner in my now less frequent nocturnal sex fantasies had started to look more and more like my wife. Occasionally, I'd wake up with a start in the dawning light, flat on my back, staring down towards the foot of the bed. My vision would be obscured by the peaked, tent-like rise of blanket about halfway down, the old tent pole stiff with lingering memories not only of dreams but of waking ecstasies. The lines of an old song played on the radio of my mind: "At night when you're asleep . . . into your tent I'll creep." When I rolled over against Loretta, snuggling like one teaspoon fitting perfectly onto another, she'd mumble something incoherent which I'd take for the usual, "Not tonight, Henry."

But usually I do not awake in mid-dream. What I've found is that as my dream fantasies become less frequent, my waking fantasies become more so. I find myself looking at women, mostly women young enough to be my daughter, and ruminating. Especially now that I'm interviewing for a new secretary for my real estate office. They bat their large blue or brown eyes at me and tell me how wonderful it must be to sell real estate in this marvellous little California suburb with so many beautiful homes. What they don't say is this *rich* little suburb with so much money floating about. Only a fool would not have thought it, and I don't think they're fools.

"I so much want to learn the business, Mr. de Anza," one says, beaming a meaningful smile at me. "I think I could learn a lot from you."

Like with most men though, my fantasies work themselves out in talk. Man talk that starts in the early teens when, in post-puberty euphoria, you first discuss your lustful thoughts with your buddies. Funny, it never seems to elevate itself much beyond that, as if your talk springs full-grown with pubic fuzz and a deepening, still uncontrollable voice. Some of us though, do become more discreet as we grow older and less prone to bragga-docio.

Where my little gang gets together is down on University Avenue at O'Hara's Coffee Shop every weekday morning at ten o'clock, business allowing, and occasional Saturdays. O'Hara's real name is Willie Jackson. He's not Irish but Black, and a good Republican who lives discreetly on the other side of the freeway in our so-called ghetto, even though this is a liberal community, and he could live anywhere he wants. If Willie weren't quite so dark one of our gang would certainly stand him up for member-ship in the Elks Club. But as it is—well, Willie doesn't mind. He understands.

O'Hara's serves watery coffee and terrible food. The waitress who's been there forever doesn't like to wear her hearing aid, and she's never learned to read lips very well. If you don't articu-late carefully, you're apt to be served an O'Hara Surprise. But then, as I said, you don't go to O'Hara's for the food. You go there for the ambience. To see all the other small businessmen in town who come in for their watery cup, holding it out like Oliver Twist asking for "more"; to trade snappy repartee with the deaf waitress; to see the local downtown characters parade in and out, and we've got some characters in this town—creeps we used to call them when I was in school. I wouldn't miss it. Morning coffee without O'Hara's is like a picnic without ants.

I didn't get to join the gang this past week. Business has been good so I've been squiring disillusioned prospects around to the overpriced houses for sale. I feel for them. Hubby gets trans-ferred from back East to Silicon Valley and wants a nice place for wifey and kids. Especially if his job means long hours or lots of travel. That's the cutting edge of where mortgages turn into conscience money. It takes awhile for the shock to wear off after I first show them around. To realize that it costs almost twice as much for a house in the San Francisco Bay area as it does for the same house in Gritville, Ohio.

So as I said, I missed the coffee club all week and didn't make it to O'Hara's until Saturday morning while Loretta was at her art gallery because her assistant was sick.

"Hey," one of the gang said. "Here he is. Too busy getting

rich on his six percent commissions to have a cup with his old friends."

I heard the pinch of malice in Jimmy's voice underlying his attempt to be funny. His shoe store isn't doing too well these days and really hasn't for a long time. Ever since the college kids started wearing sandals and then those "earth"shoes or whatever they call them, that tilt you back on your heels and probably give you curvature of the spine. Nobody buys wingtip brogans anymore except maybe a few old Stanford grads who run insurance agencies like Al, one of our gang.

I gave them a big grin as I slid into the booth and picked up the check. "Just to show you my heart's in the right place," I said. I had barely shoved an empty cup to the edge of the table when here came our waitress, coffee pot in hand, to give me the business about where had I been. Was I sick? Or did I have another girl friend now that she had a few gray hairs? A few? If you scraped away the henna it would be her whole scalp.

There were three of them at the table this morning: Jimmy, the shoe man; doom and gloom Al with his Henny Penny advice about the latest disaster for which we'd better buy a policy to protect our homes and potential widows; old Louis who was a contractor. Louis was semi-retired; the only contracting he does now other than a few repairs for old friends is for doll houses for his three granddaughters. He built a Victorian doll house for our youngest granddaughter, Kim, that is a work of art.

The gang went on with their conversation as if I had been there all along. "You mean over there on the block behind the old library?" Jimmy was saying. "They're going to tear those down?"

Louis nodded. "They're razing the whole block and putting in condos."

"How much you say they paid for those lots?" Jimmy asked. Louis gave him a figure, and Jimmy looked at me with an expression on his face to ask if that was right. I nodded, and Jimmy whistled.

"I remember," Al said in that deep, sepulchral voice of his— many's the time I thought he should have been a mortician instead of an insurance agent—"when I could have bought those lots for—" He gave a figure that was pennies on the current dollar.

Well, that started the game of "I remember," one of our favorites. I remember when that land over across from the golf course was fifty cents an acre, one said. Yeah, swamp land, someone countered. Anyway, who had fifty cents? somebody else asked.

It goes that way a lot with us—remembering. Like what was the name of the store on the corner of Emerson Street three, four, five businesses ago? Or what family built the old mansion in Crescent Park that the city recently took over as a historic building? I swear, these old guys remember everything.

"Tell me, Louis," Jimmy said, after we got through remembering for a few minutes. "You getting a piece of that condo action?"

Everybody grinned because they knew Louis wasn't. Even in his prime it would have been a bit too ambitious an undertaking for him. But instead of telling Jimmy to go to hell, Louis leaned over his coffee cup with a serious look on his face.

"What if I told you," he said, giving me a wink, "I was going to be the foreman of a bunch of those new-age carpenters who're going to build those condos? You know the type. Pony-tailed hairdos and bare feet except for those sandals they all wear. Steel-toed workshoes have gone out of style."

Jimmy got red in the face when we all laughed; he had put a pair of those steel-toed workshoes in the window of his store just last week.

Then Al looked over at me before he mounted his pulpit and made his pronouncement, nodding as if he knew a secret. "Henry," he said. "You ought to have some land that would be just right for condominiums."

I knew what he was thinking. De Anza is a old family name in these parts, going back to the Mexican land grant days. There's even a college by that name over in the nearby town of Cupertino. Because of this, everybody's always kidding me about how I must own half the county.

"No," I said, shaking my head sadly. "You gringos robbed us of all that land decades ago." They all kind of chuckled, but I could see the uneasy shift in their eyes. They don't anymore like being called gringos than I like being called Mexican—even in fun.

"All the land is in my wife's family," I said by way of apology.

She was just a little country girl from near Morgan Hill when we met at San José State University. She was going to be a great artist. Then reality cornered her and persuaded her to become an art teacher and marry me. Just a few years ago the new breed of high school students nearly drove her crazy, so she used some of her inheritance to retire from teaching and open an art gallery downtown on Ramona Street over near the Art Club building.

"We still have a few acres north of Morgan Hill that her poppa left her when he died," I said. "If the state ever gets off its ass and puts in a connector to Highway 101, we can build some homes to sell to those rich engineers down there who work at the IBM plant."

Meanwhile, Louis wasn't even listening to me. It wasn't because he already knew what I was saying. His eyes had narrowed and were riveted on someone coming up the aisle behind me. He leaned forward, his eyes still on whoever it was coming in, and said sotto voce, "Here comes the tycoon who owns the whole block."

Al, who was sitting beside him and facing the same way, raised his eyebrows in surprise. "Why I thought it would be—" He mentioned the names of the two principals of the biggest real estate firm in the area. "*He's* no developer. What's he doing with condos?"

"Who?" I said. I didn't want to turn around and stare.

"Old Rolls Royce," Louis said, and I immediately knew who he meant.

Old Rolls Royce wasn't one of the regulars. What I mean is, you never see him in O'Hara's during the week. On weekends though, he sometimes comes in in his tennis clothes or lately maybe in his jog suit. He's an old codger maybe about our age—five years or so older than me but a couple of years younger than Louis.

We only know him by the cars he drives. The latest is that gorgeous Silver Cloud Rolls sedan, but when we first noticed him he was Mr. Oldsmobile 88. He trades in cars like some women buy new lipsticks, going from Mr. Oldsmobile 88 to Mr. Buick to Mr. Cadillac until someone must have told him that Cadillacs were OK in Los Angeles but gauche in the San Francisco Bay area. The short-lived Cadillac soon became a BMW which became a Mercedes which finally became the Rolls.

"What's he do, Louis?" I asked. "Whatever it is, he makes a lot of money."

"Electronics!" Jimmy declared.

"Are you kidding?" Louis said. "Those electronics people all have PhD's and talk in three syllables. I sat in the booth next to him one Saturday, and he's strictly from the streets of 'Noo Joisey.'" Louis' New Jersey accent was lousy, but I got the idea. "Besides, most of the electronics people are a lot younger. This old guy came up the long, hard way."

But as they passed our booth it wasn't Mr. Rolls Royce that I was looking at, and I barely heard Louis say, "He's in the import business. South America. Hong Kong. His office is in San Francisco. I hear he cornered the market on raw silk from mainland China."

All I noticed was this well-shaped derriere in these silk jogging shorts, and I could tell by the firmness of the flesh that she was no contemporary of old Rolls Royce's.

Al was watching me with a tight smile on his face. "I got the best view," he said. "Looks to me like he traded in on a new model."

But I didn't hear him. I was into one of my daytime fantasies. I thought about Loretta and how we seemed to lead separate lives now. Her with her artsy-fartsy friends and me with my contractors and bank loan officers and all those crass money men. I thought about how many years it's been since either one of us had firm flesh and about which one of us had the fewest incipient liver spots.

I felt a dull ache in my lower stomach, as if there were things undreamed of that I had never tasted and time was running out. Perhaps I'd never taste them. I'd never own a Silver Cloud Rolls Royce, nor a home in Atherton or Woodside or Portola Valley. Sex would never be as sweet and hot and frequent as it used to be. I'd never again see adoring eyes across the breakfast table telling me how wonderful I was.

Stop it! I finally thought to myself. Goddamn stop it, before you break down and cry right here.

I spent the rest of my coffee break discreetly eyeballing Rolls

Royce's companion who sat facing me, the edges of her silk shorts pulled high up her thighs. It nearly drove me crazy. After I couldn't stand it anymore, I gulped down the rest of my coffee before old deaf-ear refilled my cup, and took my leave of the gang. They were talking about how much more moral everybody was in the good old days, but there was a foot-and-a-half of envy coating their cluck-cluck-clucking.

My conscience must have bothered me, because I found myself heading down Ramona Street to the gallery without consciously planning to. Loretta was talking to a customer, and she looked up in surprise and gave me a polite little smile when the door bell tinkled. She spoke at me in a breathless voice, "Enrique! I'll be with you in a moment."

At home I'm just Henry, but she calls me Enrique in the gallery because she thinks it sounds tonier. It's her Slavic childhood on the farm; her grandparents spoke one of those guttural tongues. That's why she always thought Spanish was such a beautiful language, and when we were first married she insisted that I speak only Spanish when we made love.

I looked around at the stuff hanging on the walls until the customer left. "No sale!" Loretta groused when the door slammed. "Things have really been slow this month."

"Why don't you close up and come down to the real estate office. You could type up some contracts. I still haven't found a secretary."

She arched an eyebrow as if typing contracts was the last thing in the world she'd consider. "That girl," she said, meaning her assistant. She looked at me as if deciding whether or not to tell me. "She really isn't sick," she finally said. "Her boyfriend kicked her out, and she's looking for a place to live."

I couldn't help but guffaw. "My, how things have changed since we were young. People didn't admit living together, and there weren't any such things as 'relationships.' We used to call it shacking up. Or playing house, which was sort of a grown-up version of playing doctor."

"Don't be vulgar, Henry, You're almost as bad as these young people. Standards have just deteriorated, that's what. Even among women."

I didn't want to say anything else vulgar, so I just thought it.

Women of Loretta's generation run whining to their psychiatrists about their goddamned orgasms. The new generation doesn't seem to have that problem. Orgasms are great, but housing's in short supply. Which is another way of saying loyalty or commitment. It's almost like those baseball cards I used to trade as a kid. One loyalty is worth three orgasms—or is it six? It all depends on who's doing the trading.

"Well, the generation gap is closing," I said. "At least there are a few trying to close it. Old Rolls Royce was at O'Hara's this morning with some luscious young thing in shorts and T-shirt."

"You mean—?" She mentioned what must have been his real name. "Well," she said. "His wife was in here last week trying to sell some paintings." Her mouth was open, ready to continue, when the door bell tinkled. "Later," she said, preening herself into a smile as the customer approached. With a wave, I went out into the street.

As I walked to my office it was the same damned parade, a regular side-show. Or maybe it was just that I was unusually sensitized this morning. Shorts. T-shirts. No bras. Nipples popping through thin blouses. Good grief. No wonder old men go berserk.

When I got to the office I saw evidence that my one salesman had come and gone. I shuffled through the mail, then sat down at the typewriter to hunt and peck my way through the papers I needed for Monday morning.

I was cursing and looking for the Sno-Pak to white out a mistake when the door opened behind me and a faint floral scent called me to attention.

"Good morning, Señor de Anza." I turned to see this bright smile semi-clothed in jogging shorts and I guess you'd call it a tank top. It was really a man's sleeveless undershirt with these alert boobs winking at me through the ribbed material. It was one of my secretarial applicants, the one who so much wanted to learn the business—from me.

It was difficult keeping my eyes on her face, but I managed. "Good morning—" Then my memory clicked. "Chris Lewis, isn't it?"

The smile broadened. "You remembered. I was just passing by, and I wondered if you'd decided about that job yet."

The rent must be due, I thought, or her boyfriend is going to kick her out. But somehow that didn't really matter. Her bright smile, her sheer aliveness, were balm for the ache I felt.

"There are two other applicants," I said, not telling her that I planned to make reference checks. "I hope to settle it by the middle of next week."

A little girl look of disappointment clouded her face, and she came closer in a way that made me want to reach out to comfort her. "I could come in first thing Monday morning," she said. "I'd really like it here; I can tell."

When she got uncomfortably close she peered over my shoulder at the typewriter. "Two hundred and thirty-five thousand dollars for three bedrooms, two baths. My!" Then she pulled back as if remembering herself. "I'd even help you type some of that now except that I'm on my way to the pharmacy to pick up my monthly refill of pills."

An uncertain smile twitched at her mouth, but when we made eye contact the smile stabilized, and the tip of a little pink tongue came out and glided across her lips. I started to perspire because I knew she meant "The Pill."

"Tell me, Mr. de Anza, did they name the college after you?"

"It was part of the original family grant," I lied, "a long, long time ago."

"I went there for a semester right after high school. That was a long, long time ago too. Almost ten years." Then she turned abruptly and looked at some of the listings on the bulletin board. Her voice came casually over one bare shoulder. "I thought I'd better tell you about one of my references," she said. "My last job. I had a personality conflict with the office manager, and she might not give me a good recommendation." She turned abruptly. "She was just a jealous old bitch."

I can see that, I thought, staring where I shouldn't have been staring.

"I could be in at eight o'clock Monday morning," she said.

I had to laugh at her audacity, and Chris laughed too. "All right," I said. "Let's give it a try."

She smiled and said thank you, then turned and gyrated out the door saying, "Bye-bye until Monday."

At home that evening Loretta asked me if I got my contracts

typed; she must have felt guilty about not wanting to help. I said yeah; I did them myself. Then she asked if I was ever going to find a secretary. I said soon; I had three candidates.

"Are they pretty?" she asked. No, I said. And that ended that.

What she really wanted to talk about was Mrs. Rolls Royce. She got very excited and animated when she gossiped. She knew a lot more about Mrs. R.R. than I did, what with bits and pieces of information exchanged with the local hair dresser, the sales manager of the fanciest boutique in town, and the woman dancercize instructor at the Exclusively Hers Spa whose cousin ran a fat farm in Baja California.

"It's been going on for over a year," Loretta began, and she told me the whole story.

She first became aware of it from her friend at the boutique. Old Rolls Royce came in with this young thing who wasn't his daughter and bought the shop's monthly sales quota in an hour and a half. Two days later Mrs. Rolls Royce came in like she did occasionally, but she wasn't buying that day. She wanted to go over her account, item by item, and Loretta's friend didn't know what to do. She was going to say that her records were with her accountant when Mrs. Rolls Royce pulled open the desk drawer and pulled out the book. Well, you couldn't very well snatch it away from one of your best customers.

"I see," Mrs. Rolls Royce said, running a finger down the page. "Yes," her face getting redder and redder. "What size were these that you sold day before yesterday?"

Loretta's friend did not know what to say. "What size?" Mrs. Rolls Royce almost shouted, and the shop manager blurted out size 8. Mrs. Rolls Royce looked down at her arms and her front and turned her head to check her hips as if she were using a tape measure. But she didn't need a tape measure. Nobody would imagine that a size 12 body would fit into a size 8 dress.

She thrust her red face almost nose to nose with the shop manager. "The next time he brings her in," she said, and her voice was a little hysterical, "I want you to telephone me immediately. Immediately! Do you hear?" And she spun on her heel and stomped out.

An isolated incident like that was only something juicy to share with a friend or two, then forget along with the rest of yesterday's junk news. But some weeks later, Loretta went to the Spa for a massage. It was here that she heard the next chapter.

When the dancercize class didn't seem to do whatever Mrs. R.R. wanted done for her fast enough, she went down to Baja to the fat farm for a crash course. Sort of the way a businessman might go to Berlitz to learn enough Spanish to close a deal in Mexico City. She was back now, and when the dancercize class broke, Loretta saw her come into the massage room with the usual dumpy crowd trying to do something about the accumulated years of indulgent living.

"You wouldn't have recognized her," Loretta said. "She lost twenty pounds. Blondined her hair. And it looked suspiciously like she'd had a face lift although she couldn't be much over forty-five."

In the meantime, she'd refused to give Mr. Rolls Royce a divorce. It was enough to make you wonder if they were Catholic. You still hear about that kind of attitude among old-fashioned Catholics. But we'd never seen the likes of the Rolls Royces at St. Albert the Great's or St. Thomas Aquinas. Or even the time or two when we went to St. Marcella's in Woodside or Our Lady of the Wayside's in Portola Valley. They were definitely not Catholic, Loretta said. Her friend at the Spa confirmed it.

It was about that time, too, that Mrs. R.R. began to wear those damned unfashionable jog suits that you see all over town in all shapes and sizes. Somebody said she'd been taking tennis lessons just to show her husband, but someone else said she was dating the young tennis instructor. The real story was that her *husband* was trying to get her to date the tennis instructor. Mr. R.R. was paying the instructor for more than lessons, although the young cad was collecting money for a job he wasn't doing.

As Loretta was telling me this, I remembered the woman with blondined hair whom I had seen around town. Every time I saw her she had on a different color jog suit, almost as if she had one for each day of the week. I recall wondering if on Sunday she wore her church version which would probably be white.

"Well," Loretta said. "It's obvious that he's trying to trade her in to this young jock. But women aren't automobiles. You can't sell them if they don't want to be sold."

"Why does she hang on?" I asked. "There's no question what's going on between Mr. R.R. and his young thing."

Loretta gave me a look as if this was another of my dumb questions. "Pride," she said.

"Not loyalty?"

"Well," she said. "She's not his *first* wife." I reared back in surprise. "Yes," Loretta said. "She's fifteen years younger than him. She took him away from some old woman who's now in a retirement home somewhere suffering from early senility."

"Pride?" I repeated.

"It's a battle to the death," Loretta said. "Now their estate in Woodside is up for sale. They say *she*," meaning the younger woman, "wants him to move into the City," meaning San Francisco. Then Loretta pursed her lips in thought and aimed a wrinkled brow at me. "There'll be a marvellous commission for someone."

"I don't travel in those circles," I answered. "It's enough to find homes for electronics engineers moving up to the executive suites around here."

"Anyway," Loretta said, "she's starting to sell off some of their antiques and art. She came to see me about the paintings. She's not going to leave the son-of-a-bitch a thing if she can manage. And he's going to have to call the police to drag her out of their Woodside place. It'll be a terrible scandal." She gave a funny little laugh.

"Then of course," Loretta went on. "She's starting to drink too much."

There it was. The whole background. And Loretta had known about it all along.

I got to the office a few minutes late Monday morning. My salesman gave me a wiseacre grin and nodded toward the young lady seated at the typewriter looking it over to be sure it wouldn't bite.

Later that morning, when Chris went to the restroom, he came up to me, still with that leer on his face. "She's not much of a typist, but I bet she's fun on a date."

I tried to ignore him. It just confirmed my feeling that he'd never be a crackerjack salesman and that I'd never make him my junior partner. No tact. Chris had more sense than he did; she completely ignored him.

As the days went by her typing didn't get much better, but my salesman stopped trying to hustle her when he saw how things were between Chris and me. One morning I arrived at O'Hara's a little earlier than usual and found only Jimmy waiting in our usual booth. When he saw me come past the counter and down the aisle, he grinned with that same wiseacre expression that my salesman flashed at me occasionally.

I was no more than stirring the sugar and cream in my coffee when he leaned across the table. "Quite the Lothario these days, I hear. Next thing you know you'll be ordering a Rolls Royce."

"I don't know what you're talking about," I answered.

"Aw, come on." The insipidness of his grin was exceeded only by my feeling that it was none of his business. "A little bird saw a prominent real estate man head to head with a certain young lovely in a dark corner of Qui Hing Low over in Mountain View one day last week."

"I can't imagine," I said.

Then his face turned serious. He looked over my shoulder as if he saw somebody approaching. His next words were almost a whisper. "Take a tip from an old friend," he said. "Discretion. You know the old saying: Don't get your meat where you earn your potatoes."

By then we heard Louis's greeting. I was too damned angry to do anything but glower, even when Louis asked, "What's the matter with him?" I left without finishing my cup.

I saw old Rolls Royce and his lady friend at O'Hara's once or twice more over the next couple of weekends. You couldn't tell from them that it wasn't anything but on the up and up—a long-time married couple out slumming at the local coffee shop.

Mrs. Rolls Royce and her jog suits were spotted here and there: leaving the bank, entering the post office, weaving out of one of the ladies' restaurants where she no doubt overdid the white wine.

Loretta kept me up-to-date on what she heard. Mrs. R.R. had given up tennis and the tennis pro. She made a scene one day in the city hall underground parking lot when she tried to kick in the side of a Rolls Royce. It was not her husband's; he was usually in San Francisco on weekdays. Unlucky for her the Police Department is just upstairs.

Funny thing too, I realized about then that I hadn't had one of my occasional nighttime or even daytime fantasies for quite awhile. Either that or I was no longer remembering my dreams. It was as if real life and dream life were interchangeable, and you didn't have to experience the same things in both places. Fulfillment in one life takes care of it for the other.

One Saturday I popped into O'Hara's for a quick cup before going to the office to meet Chris.

"What's this about you going down to Carmel?" Louis asked. "I thought you only handled real estate here and in San Mateo County?"

Jimmy was watching me with a sly look, and I felt my face warm to a flush. "It's a special deal," I said. "One of those rare opportunities."

Jimmy broke into a grin. "I could go down with you and be your recording secretary. I can take short hand."

It got very quiet and uncomfortable at the table but nobody said anything until I couldn't stand it. "Thanks for the offer," I finally said. "Only trouble is your legs aren't good looking enough." Everybody burst out laughing.

Just after that Al put a finger to his lips and looked down the aisle toward the front entrance. "Here comes old Rolls Royce and his young thing," he said.

"I hear Mrs. Rolls Royce won't give him a divorce," Jimmy said. "Says half of the estate isn't enough."

"Somebody told me he was going to charge her with adultery with some Stanford tennis player." Al said.

Louis looked at the young thing in jog shorts as she breezed by, wafting perfume with memories of things more exotic than jogging or tennis. "I don't understand it," Louis said uncharacteristically; the old puritan almost never commented during our sex talks. "It's all the same stuff. I can't see why one is worth a few million dollars while another isn't worth the time of day."

"You're just getting old, Louis," Jimmy said. "Isn't he, Henry?"

"It's all in the mind," Al said. "It's just the way you look at it."

"There *is* a difference," I said. They all got very quiet and listened as if they were receiving pearls straight from the guru's lips. "Otherwise why would you all be looking at her and not at old Mrs. Whitcomb?"

Mrs. Whitcomb, one of the retired widows who lived in the

apartment hotel downtown and a regular customer of O'Hara's, had just hobbled in, balancing herself as if walking a plank. I don't think anyone at the table but me had seen her enter.

About that time Rolls Royce's young lady got up from their booth and went to the back where the restrooms and the telephone were. "Got to call the racquet club to hold their court because they'll be a little late," Jimmy said. "O'Hara's fry cook has such a bad case of hangover shakes that he keeps breaking the yolks on the fried eggs."

We all had to laugh because, in addition to a deaf waitress, O'Hara's has to have one of the most inept fry cooks in California history. Even O'Hara (I mean Willie Jackson) is a better egg cook than his hired hand.

They were still laughing when I turned to look past the almost empty stools near the cash register, then down the aisle toward the entrance from University Avenue. I almost choked on my own laughter. Mrs. Rolls Royce came down the aisle in a powder blue jog suit with a canvas pouch hanging by a strap from her shoulder. I didn't even have time to alert the guys before she glided like a sleepwalker on an escalator to her estranged husband's booth which was across the aisle and two booths away.

Jimmy was slapping the table top, still laughing about O'Hara's fry cook, while Al was wiping the corners of his eyes with a forefinger.

The Rolls Royces didn't say a word. They just stared at each other like two cats facing off. Then, almost as if in slow motion, she undid the tie to her pouch, unzipped the top, and reached in. It seemed to me as if the whole thing took a year and a half, so distinct was each motion, so deliberate each act.

"BOOM!"

It was like a cannon had gone off in my ear. Old Rolls Royce reared against the back of the padded seat as if he had been thrown by a giant. Then he fell forward, his head and chest hitting the table and sending teaspoons, coffee cups, sugar container, and creamer scattering onto the floor.

For an instant everything in the coffee shop stopped. Mrs. Rolls Royce turned and passed the counter, placing the smoking revolver beside a plate as if she was leaving a fifty-cent tip for the waitress. Then, in this awful silence, she walked down the aisle and out the door as calm as you please.

The first one to scream was Mrs. Whitcomb, who sat directly behind Rolls Royce's booth. The busboy dropped a tray, and you could hear him hollering in Spanish above the metallic clatter as the tray rolled across the floor. Rolls Royce's young thing rushed from the back and peered into the coffee shop proper. Her face turned white, and she pressed a knuckle against her open mouth before she slumped to the floor.

There must have been a pair of police officers having coffee in back because I saw one blue uniform rush to Rolls Royce's table while a second blue uniform ran down the aisle to the front entrance. But Mrs. Rolls Royce wasn't going anywhere. She was standing on the sidewalk waiting, as if she knew that the policemen were in there. When the officer burst through the door, she held out her two wrists for the bracelets.

The place was bedlam now. I felt faint and moist all over. I half rose in my seat and looked over the low partition that separated booths. Rolls Royce wasn't moving a tic. The blood pulsed onto the table top, oozing into the puddle of cream-lightened coffee. All I could think was: How will I ever eat catsup again?

It could have been two minutes or two hours, I don't know, but eventually an ambulance sirened its way there, with its sibling police siren right behind. There was nothing they could do. She was a hell of a shot. They took our names and addresses and what information anyone could stammer out.

We sat there afterwards, stone silent, trying to calm down enough to leave. After a bit Louis and Al and Jimmy went out the back and across the alley to the place that had a bar that opened early for the local wino trade.

Somehow I staggered the three blocks to the art gallery. It was the longest three blocks I ever walked. I pushed through the door, then sank onto one of Loretta's fancy chairs. She had heard the tinkle and come from the back smiling expecting to see a customer. When she saw me, her face dropped a foot.

"My God!" she said. "What happened to you?"

"She killed him," I mumbled. "Shot him right through the heart."

"Speak up! I can't understand you."

Then the hairdresser from next door rushed in, shouting and drowning out the bell. "She shot him dead! Right there in the middle of O'Hara's. I told you, Loretta. I told you!" She nodded, not even noticing me. "I've got to rush down to the boutique and tell her, too." She was gone as quickly as she had come, the town crier on her mission.

Loretta watched her hurry away, jaywalking diagonally across the street. Then Loretta looked down and saw me slumped there, all in, and you could see the lightbulb go on inside her head. "You were there," she said.

She turned and hurried to her enclosed office, then hurried back with a bottle of sherry and one of her fancy cut classes. "Here," she said, thrusting a glassful at me.

I tossed it off in one gulp and waited for it to go down and start numbing me. Loretta sat on the chair beside me. "My God! Tell me all about it."

Telling anybody all about it was the last thing I wanted to do. I wanted to be still and try to digest what had happened. Her gossip-eager face irritated me, and I wished she could see what bad shape I was in.

"Mrs.—?" and she said Mrs. Rolls Royce's real name. I nodded. "I knew it. I just knew it. Did she get away?"

When I shook my head, Loretta's expression hardened. "Too bad. I hope they let her off. The bastard deserved it." Then she turned and stared me straight in the eyes. "You know what the marriage vows say: Till death do us part."

"Till death do us part," I managed to mumble.

"Exactly!" There was a viciousness to her voice as if the word was an assault—or was it a threat? "Why must women always have to bear the burden because of their sex?"

I looked at her, sensing her caged up rage and feeling a chilling fear that turned into trembling. Women aren't the only ones burdened by their sex, I thought. Men have their burdens too, the greatest one being how to transcend being ruled by their glands. Women don't have that problem. Not many of them. While most men do.

"He got what he deserved," she repeated. "Good for her!"

I was trembling uncontrollably, but she hadn't even noticed. Deep down I acknowledged something I had always known but never really wanted to admit: I would always be lonely—and alone, even though the closest I have ever come to escaping it was in rare moments with Loretta.

I thought of that rich bastard with the hole in his chest. I thought of Mrs. Rolls Royce on her way to jail. I thought of Loretta. I also thought of Chris, who would finally leave the office in a snit when I didn't show up and whom I would fire next week.

Who is the prisoner of whom in this mad merry-go-around? I thought. If the prisoner and the jailer are manacled to each other, does it matter who is called what? For one to be truly liberated, the other must be too. Mrs. Rolls Royce is no freer than her dead husband. While I am no more nor no less Loretta's prisoner than I am Chris' jailer.

A terrible sadness came over me as I sat there inundated by Loretta's chatter. Till death do us part, I thought—one way or another. I looked up at her, and it was like watching a mime. Her lips moved, but I didn't hear a thing.

Affirmative Action

Next to having her husband, Antonio, alive again, what Rosalia Soto wanted most of all was a place of her own. She had been forced to sell their little house in the Los Angeles barrio of Boyle Heights when Antonio's insurance failed to cover the hospital bill for his fatal bout with cancer. Now she was a permanent guest—she could not really call it her home—in her youngest daughter's house.

Not only did she lack a sense of control over her own life, she also lacked privacy which had become a necessity rather than a luxury as she grew older. Finally, there was her grandson Pancho's new wife, a gringa who brought an alien intrusion into the already crowded house. It was enough to weigh down the sturdiest soul.

This afternoon, like most afternoons at three o'clock, she retreated to her room that contained the remnants of her earlier, independent life. The large, round mirror on the 1930s Hollywood-style dresser reflected her short, stout body sacked in a black widow's dress. She did not give her reflection a thought; she did not care what she looked like. The bureau, a companion piece to the mahogany veneer dresser, was cracked in the upper right corner where her sons-in-law dropped it while moving.

Rosalia stretched out on the bed with matching headboard, the bed which she once shared with Antonio and now shared with her youngest granddaughter. She dared not look at Antonio's framed photograph on the bureau. She knew it would make her cry. She would just close her eyes for a few minutes until the younger children came home from school, and the older members of the household came home from work.

Enjoy the quiet while you can, she thought. Soon the TV set in the living room will go on; one of the back rooms will turn into urban cowboy with that honky-tonk Texas music; another room will vibrate to cha-cha, ranchero, mariachi boom-boom; while out front some high school boy will park his auto stereo with wheels, playing that electric rock music that makes my hair stand on end. No wonder nobody talks anymore, she thought. They can't get a word in edgewise. The noise machines have taken over.

She had barely closed her eyes when the too-polite, bootlicking voice called through the closed door. "Mama? Are you in there, Mama?"

"Yes. What is it this time?"

The door opened a crack, and her daughter, María, poked only her face into private territory. An envelope extended tentatively, like an immigrant waiting for permission from the Border Patrol to cross the line.

"Your Social Security check came," María said. But her voice told Rosalia that there was more; that the check was not the real reason she was here.

"Put it on the dresser."

As María put the envelope down, an expression of pain crossed her face. "Oh, Mama. You look so sad."

Tears of rage welled up in Rosalia's eyes, but she willed them away. I don't know which is worse, she thought. To be pitied by María or to fight with my other daughter, Stella, who is stubborn, malicious, and selfish. "What is it you want?" she snapped.

María's face paled, the look from her childhood when she had bad news: a poor grade on her report card or being late to Mass. "Pancho and Maureen are bringing her father over for dinner tonight."

María stood with her elbows against her side, forearms out horizontally, hands hanging limply, like a dog on its hind legs begging for a bone. Rosalia groaned.

"They're moving out this weekend," María explained hurriedly. Rosalia already knew that. "They have their own little apartment near the aircraft plant," she added brightly. Rosalia already knew that too. "As long as Panchito doesn't get laid off—" Her voice trailed into silence as if she hoped that her mother would not hear this last.

"I'll be there," Rosalia said, meaning dinner.

"Do you think . . . " Here it comes, Rosalia thought. Oh,

Lord, save me from timid hearts. " . . . you could make a nice batch of flour tortillas for dinner? You know how Mr. Fitzpatrick loves them."

Rosalia sat upright and nodded angrily, thinking: Yes. I'll put ground glass and rat poison in the batch for that old fart.

María left, but there was no use resting now. Rosalia looked up at the photograph on the dresser and felt the immense emptiness in her life.

She was back in Boyle Heights again, where she and Antonio had moved when they first married and left Arizona. Where they had raised their family the way they were supposed to be raised. Where one could walk the streets and be in Mexico, surrounded by happy brown faces. Inhaling the fragrance of pozole and oregano from the cafes and delicatessans. Hearing the soft, beautiful sounds of their own Spanish language.

But then children grew up and did not appreciate what their parents had done for them. Boyle Heights wasn't good enough anymore. "Oh, Mama. Who wants to live in this old dump? There are beautiful new houses in Rosemead and Pico Rivera."

Rosemead? What was Rosemead? A strip of wasteland along a freeway that some rich gringo developer plastered and painted and named a fancy name to tempt dummies like María and Stella. Now they were over their heads in debt, their simple husbands chained to their jobs like monkeys tied to organ grinders. She even had to lend María and Ernesto the down payment, which was one of the many reasons she was here instead of with one of her sons.

Then, of course, moving out of Boyle Heights had been more than children rejecting what their parents taught them. It was rejecting their heritage. There, the clerks in the supermarket spoke Spanish. Here English—in the drugstore, the department store, at the movies. Even the priest here was a gringo. And with all that revolution of Pope John's, they didn't even say Mass in Latin anymore. Turning to the left and turning to the right to greet your pew mates in church was silly. Just silly. What was the world coming to?

Like my simple grandson, Pancho, she thought. What would you expect? When María told me he was getting married, I was thrilled. Until I heard he was marrying this Irish girl. ¡María santísima! It just goes to show you what happens when you don't stay with your own kind. Irish. I didn't know there were other people as dumb as us Mexicans. Otherwise how could you figure it?

Rosalia wiped her eyes and straightened her dress before going to the kitchen. The flour, lard, and rolling pin were already laid out, as if María wanted her to know what a good daughter she was.

Later the doorbell rang. It was too early for Pancho and Maureen. As the door opened, Rosalia heard the hated voice that almost at once broke into song. "Mexi . . . cali Ro . . . se," carried from the living room to the kitchen, warning her to stay put.

"Mama," María called. "Mr. Fitzpatrick is here."

For a moment Rosalia's eyes took on a life of their own, beaming at the cupboard door beneath the sink. What would a sprinkle of Drano do to the tortillas and that old lecher's stomach?

Shortly after the young people arrived. Pancho and Maureen worked at the same aircraft plant. That's where they met. Pancho was a draftsman, and Maureen was a messenger girl who carried blueprints from place to place on roller skates.

Now that there were chaperones, Rosalia could go safely in the presence of old Fitzpatrick. At dinner she purposely sat across the table from him out of foot and arm range. You know what they used to say, she thought: He's not pure Irish. He's got Russian hands and Roman fingers.

At the wedding reception he had trapped her in the kitchen when no one was looking. That's when he had let it slip that he wasn't a widower at all, but had a wife in a convalescent home who was senile and needed constant looking after.

"Well," old Fitzpatrick said to Ernesto. "The boogies are moving in everywhere. Why just this week down at work—"

Rosalia remembered when she and Antonio were foolish enough to look for a place outside of Boyle Heights and had even rented one for a short time, until they learned about the petition going around the neighborhood. "No Mexicans wanted," it had said, with all those signatures on it. She had been heartbroken and insisted that they move back to Boyle Heights even if they lost a month's rent.

"I was taking the jackhammer out to the city truck when this big boogie comes up all smiles and white teeth," Fitzpatrick said as Ernesto nodded solemnly. "'Well,' I think. 'New muscle to help out this old man.' But good God no. Not even a truck driver. He's our new foreman. Can you beat that?"

She tuned out and looked the other way at Pancho and Maureen who were playing kissy-kissy right there at the table. Soon dinner was over and old Fitzpatrick started to coo at her like that old Irish actor in one of those movies that were so popular in the 1940s. When they left the table for the living room, he got her alone long enough to whisper in her ear.

"How about it?" he said. "You've been a widow almost two years, and I've been a widower even longer. There are some things that aren't natural for humans to do without."

Her face flamed like the head of a match scraped across sandpaper. She turned and rushed into the kitchen, furious. "Mexi . . . cali Ro . . . se" pursued her like an evil spirit, out-of-tune not even the right lyrics.

María, Pancho, and Maureen stopped their huddled conversation in mid-word and looked up, but Rosalia could not be bothered about their secrets. "Coffee," she said and poured a cup.

When she carried it into the front room, old Fitzpatrick was sitting on the adjustable lounger giving Ernesto the business. "You Spanish people are the salt of the earth." Spanish indeed, Rosalia thought. Mexican! And proud of it. Then Fitzpatrick saw her and his old goat eyes lit up. "Coffee? You must have been reading my mind."

While he sat beaming, she took careful aim. She planned it so it would spill onto his lap in just the right place. If his thing hadn't shriveled up already, it would soon be scalded. Then he wouldn't go around molesting sweet old ladies.

His scream brought everyone running from the kitchen. Rosalia was all horrors and apologies. Then, after Maureen brought a dish towel to wipe her father's lap, Rosalia worked up a few tears. On the pretext of being upset, she excused herself to go to her room . . . for a little peace and quiet. No more "Mexacali Rose." Hopefully never again.

On Saturday, moving day, Pancho and Maureen slept in. There was a listless sense of disappointment in the air, and María avoided her mother. Finally, when no one else got up for breakfast and there was only the two of them across the table, María wiped at her dry, red eyes and spoke in a trembling voice.

"Pancho is being laid off," she said. "The government is not renewing some contract, and the people without seniority are being let go first."

"What about Maureen? If they don't need draftsmen, they surely don't need roller derby."

María shook her head with fast, tiny little movements that resembled trembling more than saying no. Then the tears started.

"What do you mean?" Rosalia's voice rose. "It's prejudice! They're doing it to us again, and it's against the law!"

María dripped tears onto her toast, and little pipsqueak sounds came from deep in her throat. She stood abruptly, almost knocking over the table, and rushed out of the kitchen. Rosalia was left with spilled coffee, tear-sogged toast, and egg yolks congealing on a cold plastic plate.

She cleared the table and sat down alone for another cup of coffee. It was so quiet for a change. Ernesto had long since gone to work. The young people were making up for the sleep they had traded for playtime last night. María must be crying in her room, although it was such a timid cry that it couldn't be heard in the kitchen. If circumstances had been better, the rare early morning quiet would have been enjoyable.

A sound of footsteps. Not María's pussyfooting but the slap of bare feet on linoleum. Then *she* appeared in some kind of wrap that you could almost see through.

"Morning, Grandma Rosalia."

Maureen went to the stove and poured herself a cup of coffee, then plopped down at the table. Rosalia felt a strange apprehension. It was not fear, but an uncertainty that she felt with so many of these young creatures today. They weren't like she was when she was young. She didn't understand them. Then, too, she and Maureen had seldom been alone together in the three months the young bride had lived there. This thought surprised the old lady.

Maureen sighed and took a sip from her cup. "Did María tell you about Ricky?" Rosalia nodded. Then the girl's face turned

red, and she glared intently with beady green eyes, thrusting her
head forward aggressively. "I told him he was a fool to let them
do that to him. I wouldn't put up with it. In fact, I didn't."

"You're not getting laid off?" Rosalia remembered María's
trembling head that had already answered that question, but
sometimes María got things wrong.

"They tried to." The girl flashed an impish smile. "When my
supervisor told me, I went right to the Personnel Department
and set them straight."

Then her mood shifted. Rosalia could almost see the change
on her face, like watching a TV screen when the channel selector
was turned.

"I want my own place," she said adamantly. "Ricky and I need
some privacy. I'm twenty years old, and I've never had a place of
my own. There's always been Papa. And Mama when she was
well."

"Do you need money?"

Maureen's expression answered: What a silly question. "We
had the cutest little apartment picked out. With a swimming pool
and sauna and everything." Then she blinked, lips compressed.
"But we both have to work. Now this."

Rosalia looked at the blond young creature, at her freckles
and her youth. In her wildest dreams she would never had believed that she had anything as important as a place of one's own
in common with this daughter of that wretched old Irishman.

"I know how you feel," Rosalia said. The girl looked up in
surprise that *anyone* would know that. When you're young, no
one else in the world has your problems. Only you were chosen
by God to suffer. And strangely, when you got older, it was the
exact same thing.

Rosalia reached out and patted the girl's arm. "I could let you
have a little money," she said. She was surprised to hear the
words coming from her own mouth.

Maureen returned the pat. "Oh, Grandma. No. I wasn't asking for money." A look of stubborn determination crossed her
face. "I told Ricky he'd better do what I did. Go to Personnel.
With the two of us working we can manage it. We don't plan to
have any children for a long time." Her eyes riveted on Rosalia,
watching for any reaction. "I'm on the pill."

Ay, Dios, Rosalia thought. May the Pope have his fingers in

his ears when she talks like that. Does María know? Of course not. She'd have eight kinds of fits, and ask old Father O'-what's-his-name to come over and threaten the young people with ever-lasting damnation.

"What could Pancho do about work?" Rosalia asked, sidestepping the pill.

"Exactly what I did. They have this Affirmative Action Officer at the plant, see. He's there to make sure the company carries out the government's rules. If they don't—trouble. No more contracts."

Rosalia did not understand. If the company broke a government rule and laid Pancho off, they'd lose their contracts. If they lost their contracts, Pancho wouldn't have a job anyway. It didn't make sense.

"So when my supervisor gave me two weeks' notice, I marched right over to Personnel to the Affirmative Action Officer.

"'Look,' I said. 'I just got my notice, and I don't like it one bit.'

"He smiled a tight little smile like he's sympathizing with me. All those Personnel finks practice that smile when what they're really smiling about is that it's you and not them getting laid off.

"'One of our major contracts wasn't renewed,' he said. 'We have to reduce staff by five percent. We start by seniority, and unfortunately our younger workers are affected first. There'll be another job for—'

"But I didn't want to hear this. Five percent bullshit! A hundred percent as far as I'm concerned. 'Look,' I interrupted him. 'My last name is Mendoza, and I'm an endangered species. If I get laid off it's because my supervisor is prejudiced, and I'm going over to the Federal office in L.A. and not only report this, but sue your ass off.'

"Well, he couldn't swallow that smile fast enough. 'Mendoza?' he said. 'You don't look—'

"That made me mad, and I interrupted him again. 'Don't give me that I-don't-look crap,' I said. 'You're just proving to me your own prejudice.' Which really drove him up the wall because he's Black, see." She smiled a wicked smile, her father's smile.

"But how can you do that?" Rosalia asked. "Your name's really not Mendoza."

Maureen rolled her eyes up at the ceiling, and there was a

glint of anger in them when she glared at the old lady. "It is so," she insisted. "Sanctified by the priest and God and the state of California. My children, when I have them, will be Mendozas. Mexican by name and half-Mexican by blood. Who has a better claim?"

Rosalia was taken aback by her audacity, but she could not disagree with her logic. "So they gave you your job back?"

Maureen shook her head impatiently. "Better." She started to laugh. "They want me to be a clerk in the Affirmative Action office. They think I'll be a good 'advocate,' whatever that is. I told them I'd think about it. Actually I'd rather work on roller skates; it's much more fun. But whatever, they'll find me a job."

Rosalia marvelled at this young thing who she thought was as dumb as Pancho. Her grandson got lucky when he found her. "Good for you," she said. "Stand up for your rights."

The girl smiled. Open, warm, friendly. "I wanted to tell you. Ricky thinks the world of you. You're the only one around here who would understand and not go around wringing your hands and worrying."

Rosalia was shocked that such a daughter could come from that old fossil, Fitzpatrick, while what she had to show for a daughter was María. She watched the girl pop a frozen strawberry tart into the toaster and pour them both another cup of coffee. What would happen, Rosalia wondered, if someone brought Maureen a signed petition that said she couldn't live here? She'd tear it up and throw it in their faces, then rent the place next door and bring in her old father and some of his disreputable cronies to liven up the neighborhood. She could just see it.

There was a pussyfoot pitter-pat from the hall, and María stole in with a timid smile. "I see you girls are having a chin feast," she said, waiting by the door to be invited into her own kitchen. "Is there half a cup of lukewarm coffee left for me?"

Maureen flashed Rosalia a warning look, while María went to the stove and poured her own coffee.

"Actually," Maureen said, "we were talking about what Ricky is going to do on Monday to get his job back. Grandma agrees that it's the right thing."

The girl's smile was angelic as she pulled the hot tart from the toaster with the tips of thumb and forefinger and dropped it onto a paper towel on the table. Rosalia smiled too. María sat with a worried look on her face. Then finally she smiled, though as usual she did not know why.

This young creature is not really so different from me, Rosalia thought. I wish that I could help her more. I pray that Pancho gets his job back. That soon they'll move into their little apartment with swimming pool and sauna. She is, after all, my granddaughter. And I have had my own place, while she never has.

Kissing the Gorilla

Amelia Ruiz turned her worried face away from her husband in his wheelchair toward the entrance to the private dining room. Her right hand rested warmly on the back of his cashmere jacket, and she could hear his rasping breath and feel the bony body shudder.

For just a moment, the two brothers near the entrance stood side by side, watching the guests sign in and looking for signs of their father, the guest of honor. Their cousin from Chicago flashed the instant camera as each person advanced to the head of the line, laying the still developing dark squares of film on the open guest book, while an old family friend handed out glue-backed name tags to write on with one of several felt-tip pens.

The brothers stood stiffly, formally, in their dark Sunday suits, one blue, one black. Above their ample pot-bellies and beneath their thinning gray hair, their limpid puppy eyes were saying, "Love me. Love me."

Then the brothers parted, the quiet, watchful interlude like the brief, fleeting brush of a kiss between strangers who once were friends, meeting unexpectedly and uncertainly after too many years. Arturo, the host, rushed to the head table that was inundated with flowers, grimly shuffling through the notes clasped in his left hand. Father Tom turned and surveyed the few who had already entered, his shining clerical collar partially obscured by the inevitable effects of gravity and time on well-fed jowls.

"I told Arty," Mrs. Ruiz said, standing beside one of many tables set for six, "that they had better warn the old man. What if Manny has a heart attack when he walks in?" She spoke more to the middle-aged couple standing to her left than to her white-haired husband. She smoothed the neck of her mink stole and turned toward him. "Have you taken your pills yet, Johnny?"

"Not until I get something to eat," Mr. Ruiz said irritably. "The doctor said to take them with food or milk." She watched him look around nervously at the slow trickle of entering luncheon guests. First they paid respects to Arturo who stood, notes in one hand and a glass of something undiluted with water in the other, then they looked awkwardly around the room, eyes brightening, corners of mouths lifting, as they nodded in relief at familiar faces and moved uncertainly toward empty tables.

"Well, the sooner we sit down, the sooner we eat," Mrs. Ruiz said, removing the stole from her shoulders and draping it across the back of the chair. She sneaked a peek at the name tags of the couple beside her. "Tell me, Francis—"

The younger man had been reading the engraved invitation: "The Silva Family requests the pleasure of your company for the celebration of the 100th Birthday of Manuel Silva . . ." He slipped the card into the pocket of his suit coat. "Francisco," he said, glancing knowingly toward his wife. "I prefer Francisco."

"Tell me . . . Francisco . . . how do you come to know the Silvas?"

"Arturo and I were schoolmates. We're oldest friends. I was five when we first met. Almost fifty years ago."

"Ah," she said. "Boyle Heights."

Francisco flashed his wife another knowing look. Mrs. Ruiz realized that on the one hand she had started to use the Anglicized version of his name, and then on the other hand had assumed he had grown up in the barrio. It was all so confusing these days. "No. Southwest Los Angeles. Sixty-first Street."

"Did you hear that, Johnny?" she said to her husband. "Sixty-first Street. Why, you must have lived right around the block from my parents. Tom—Tomás," she corrected herself, "and I were childhood sweethearts." She smiled. "Isn't this a small world?"

They sat, the four of them somewhat more at ease now, the couples talking to their spouses in low voices as the room started to fill. Johnny sat stiffly in his wheelchair, his face tired and fearful, watching the waiters bustle to the tables with open bottles of California wine but no food. Finally, a waiter deposited a basket of rolls and a dish of butter on the table.

Mrs. Ruiz pounced on the basket and offered it to her husband, who took a roll and placed it on his bread plate. "Butter?" Francisco's wife asked, extending the dish.

Johnny recoiled in horror. "Cholesterol!" he said, as if she should know better. "The doctor has me on a strict diet."

"Eat your nice roll," Mrs. Ruiz said. "Then you can take your pills." She was watching him with concern, seeing the haggard look on his grayish face, a sign that he had been enduring pain for too long.

"I didn't eat any breakfast," he complained. "I thought they were going to serve lunch promptly at twelve o'clock."

"I haven't seen Tomás in thirty years," Francisco said, embarrassed by the obviously ill man. "Not since Arturo's first marriage." He turned to Mrs. Ruiz and smiled awkwardly. "I was an usher. Tomás performed the ceremony." Then he turned to his wife. "Have you ever met Tomás? I forgot." She shook her head, munching on a roll spread thick with butter, followed by a sip of white wine.

"Well, I never imagined when we were in Herbert Hoover Junior High that he would go on to Mount Carmel High School and then to the seminary," Mrs. Ruiz said. "He was such a lively little fellow. Full of the dickens."

Francisco's eyes widened. He turned their sparkling surprise on the Ruizes. "Herbert Hoover? I went to Herbert Hoover. We lived three blocks from Herbert Hoover."

"My first restaurant was just around the corner," Johnny said. "That was before I went into the tamale business. You should see the neighborhood now. Pawnshops. Soul food. Steel bars across store fronts at night."

"John D. Ruiz," Mrs. Ruiz explained, "the tamale king. Have you heard of him? Our commercials are on TV." Francisco smiled noncommittally.

"Arturo on the other hand," Mrs. Ruiz said, "was more than full of the dickens. He was wild." She leaned over the table and whispered so they could barely hear. "Manny even forgave him when he lost their house. Remember that old house in Inglewood?" She glanced around cautiously. "Manny signed it over after Arturo promised to take care of them the rest of their lives. Then Arturo's first wife caught him running around with—" She nodded toward the woman seated at the head table beside the nervous Arturo. "He lost it in the divorce settlement. Lost custody of the children, too. They're here today. With *their* children. But not his ex-wife."

She placed another roll onto Johnny's plate. "What is Arturo doing now?" she asked. Although the answer was yet to come, there was already disapproval in her manner.

"Real estate I think. I don't know for sure."

"Not selling used cars or anything . . . not quite nice?"

Francisco shrugged. "Real estate I heard."

"And what do you do?" Her eyes under arched brows watched expectantly.

"I'm an engineer."

"Didn't Arturo try that once?" Again Francisco shrugged. "Maybe he was a draftsman. Something. Yes. He tried to borrow some money to develop an invention. What was it, Johnny? Something crazy."

The sick man's eyes barely flickered. "A machine for road construction. If the operator pulled the two control levers a certain way, the machine would go out of control and shake apart. He told me there was no problem. All you had to do was hire one-armed operators. I didn't lend him the money."

The dining room had finally filled. Two oriental women, looking like mother and daughter, stood in the center of the room eyeing the two empty chairs at the table and talking in undertones. They approached, smiles straining, to ask if the places were free. Introductions all around. Amelia and Johnny Ruiz. Francisco and María Bernal. Stella and Kim Wong.

Then Arturo came bustling from the head table. "There you are, amigo," he said to Francisco. "I've been looking all over for you. Amelia. Johnny. How nice to see you. Dad will be thrilled that you came all the way from the desert."

He turned from the Ruizes to the Bernals and back. "Have you met? Francisco is one of my oldest friends." His face brightened. "A scientist," he bragged. "Satellites and space ships and that sort of thing." He clapped Francisco on the shoulder. "Amelia used to live down the block in the old neighborhood. Johnny is one of dad's dearest friends. I heard you had an operation, Johnny. How you doing?"

"As well as can be expected," Johnny said. He shook his head as a waiter approached, ready to pour from a bottle of wine. "Medication," he whispered, and the waiter moved on.

"Listen," Arturo said. "I gotta go. Pop will be here any minute. Mom will be here too. Her nurse is bringing her from the convalescent home. Jesus, I'm nervous. I have to be the master of ceremonies for this fiesta. Look!" He thrust out a trembling hand to show them. "I better get back. I'll see you afterwards. You're coming to the house, aren't you?" He left before they could nod yes.

Kim was explaining to Mrs. Bernal that she worked for Arturo who managed a florist shop downtown; their specialties were weddings and funerals.

"Here he comes," someone at the next table said excitedly.

Eyes turned toward the entrance where Manny Silva's oldest grandson held onto his upper arm and led him into the dining room.

"Arturo told me that he can handle it," Mrs. Ruiz whispered. "I hope so."

The white-haired old man moved slowly, almost as if he were balancing on a tightrope high above the ground. His tiny, delicate frame stopped just beyond the table set up in the entryway, and the camera winked at him. Everyone in the room seemed to stop breathing as if the still air made it easier for him to advance. He tilted back his head and peered from behind the lenses of his spectacles, thick as magnifying glasses, and smiled a wry smile. His lips moved, but the sound did not carry. The group at the table nearest to him laughed.

"What did he say? What did he say?"

"He said, 'Where are the dancing girls?' the old devil."

Then the applause began. A few guests rose to their feet, then the others followed, the applause building to a thunderous wave that seemed powerful enough to blow the little man over.

Tom and Arturo raced toward him, reaching him in a tie. They gingerly took him from the grandson and carefully led him across the room to the head table.

"I wish my kids cared that much," Johnny grumbled.

Amelia Ruiz patted Johnny's hand affectionately. "Doesn't he look wonderful?"

Finally, Manny Silva was seated beside Arturo. Only then did

Amelia see Mrs. Silva beside him, with Father Tom on the other side of her. "There she is," she said, pointing. "See? In the wheelchair? Poor thing. She's blind."

Mrs. Silva sat quietly, the dead sockets staring out at nothing, her thin face as translucent as bone, weighed down by her prominent nose.

"Ladies and gentlemen," Arturo began. "Thank you for coming this afternoon. Some from distant places: Chicago, Tucson, Palm Springs." He paused and nodded toward Amelia and Johnny. "Of course, you all know why we're here." Laughter erupted. "I know you must be starving by now." Again laughter; a few cheered and clapped. "So we'll make this short and have the real ceremony after we've eaten." He looked toward the entrance to the dining room. "Are we all set out there?"

The gorilla dressed in a pink tutu rollerskated between tables toward the speaker, accompanied by gasps and laughter from the crowd. It skid to a skillful stop and extended across the table the bouquet of balloons that floated in its hairy right paw. "Happy birthday, Manny," the gorilla said.

Arturo took the bouquet and slowly rotated the strings so the imprinted words were visible. "Happy," stated the red balloon. "Birthday," read the white balloon. "Manny," said the blue balloon. He handed the string of the blue balloon to his father and let the rest float to the ceiling where they bobbed politely. Then he and Tom led their father around the end of the table to the chair beside the gorilla.

"How does it feel to be a hundred years old?" the gorilla asked.

"Not like it used to."

When the laughter faded, the gorilla coyly nuzzled up to the seated old gentleman. "I have a special surprise for you," the gorilla said. It turned its masked, hairy face toward the guests, then back to Manny. "Have you ever been kissed by a gorilla?"

Without missing a beat, the old man said, "Some of them might as well have been."

The gorilla planted a hairy kiss on Manny's cheek to the accompaniment of applause and laughter. Then it turned, pulled a small silver pitch pipe from under its tutu, and blew. "All together now," it shouted. "Happy birthday to you—"

When they finished singing, the gorilla skated from the

room, and Arturo and Tom led Manny back to his place at the
table. "All right everybody," Arturo said. "Luncheon is served."

"Doesn't he look wonderful," Amelia said to Johnny. She
turned to Francisco and María. "He always was a man with a
sense of humor."

The waiter first brought the salads, followed by the entree:
filleted chicken layered with ham and covered with cheese sauce.
"I can't eat that," Johnny protested. "Doctor's orders." Amelia
beckoned to the waiter, and the three of them had a whispered
conversation about a vegetable plate. The pain on Johnny's face
deepened as he watched the others wolf down their food. "I just
got out of the hospital," he explained to Francisco.

"Shhh," Amelia said. "We're eating."

They quietly attacked their food, all except Johnny who
picked at his special vegetable plate without interest. Afterwards,
when the coffee and small hot fudge sundaes were brought
around, he shook his head and sipped water.

"A hundred years old," Johnny said, as they started to clear
the dishes. "At least I've seen three score and ten—barely—but
I'll never see a hundred. Not even four score. God! I wouldn't
miss Manny's party for the world."

Amelia patted his hand warmly. "You ate real good, dear.
Are the pills helping yet?"

"I had a bypass three years ago," Johnny said to Francisco.
"They still can't keep my blood pressure down. Then this last
operation."

"Manny had a cholostomy," Amelia said as if trying to console
Johnny. "And cataracts removed."

"And a hip joint replaced," Johnny added grimly.

Francisco twitched a smile and turned his chair so it faced the
head table where Arturo stood talking to his wife on one side and
his brother on the other. "They're about to begin," he said.

First came introductions of a few select guests who stood so
others could see them. Then the speeches began, from "Unac-
customed as I am—" to "Seriously, folks," the brothers each
taking turns philosophizing about the ages of man and telling
old stories about the guest of honor.

"As you know," Arturo said. "Pop always worked hard all his
life." His voice rose in playful mockery, and he shrugged. "Never
made much money, but he worked hard. I didn't see much of

him when I was a kid. This was during the Depression, when he worked as many as three jobs at a time, just to make ends meet.

"But you all know pop. He's always had a terrific sense of humor. That's probably why he's lived so long. Anyway, on one of these part-time jobs of his he was—" Arturo laughed uneasily. "I guess today you'd call it a custodial engineer."

"Broom jockey," the old man piped.

"Anyway, he was the . . . broom jockey . . . two days a week at the local Jewish temple. One day the rabbi comes up to him and says, 'Manuel,' in Spanish no less. Smart people those Jews. 'Manuel,' he says, 'how come a good Roman Catholic like you works in a synagogue?' "

"Well, pop was never at a loss for words. 'I'll tell you, Rabbi Goldman,' he says. 'I figure that if the devil ever comes looking for me, the last place he'd look for a good Catholic is in a Jewish temple.' " The guests roared.

Johnny turned toward María. "We were in the Knights of Columbus together," he said. "For over twenty years. Until Amelia and I moved out to the Valley."

Then the mariachis trooped in, playing "Las Mañanitas." They stopped in front of the table, and the leader handed Manny an undersized guitar. The mariachis stood in silence while he soloed the tune.

"He used to paint too," Johnny said. "Did you ever see the portrait he did of me for my fiftieth birthday?" Francisco and María shook their heads.

"He made you cross-eyed," Amelia said. "He always was better at music than he was at art."

When the guitar interlude was over, Manny stayed standing for his turn to speak. "My sons told all my good stories," he said. But he proceeded to tell about growing up on a ranch in New Mexico; of meeting the legendary Elfego Baca, toughest lawman in the West bar none—eat your heart out Wyatt Earp; of moving to California as a young man when his father lost the ranch.

"That's when I met the young lady who has meant so much to me," he said, turning toward Mrs. Silva.

She sat like a statue, her wheelchair pushed up against the edge of the table, a drool of vanilla ice cream trailing down the left side of her mouth. Her sightless eyes were immobile. The corners of her mouth moved almost imperceptibly. Suddenly

the quavering voice lashed out in what must have been a shout
for her. "Speak louder!" Indulgent smiles rolled like a gentle
wave across the room.

Manny finished by reciting the Gettysburg Address and the
Preamble to the Constitution. His display of memory was a fitting introduction to the proclamations that followed. The mayor
of the suburban city, one of the Anglos present that nobody
knew and a woman yet, read an official letter. Then Arturo read
congratulations from the President of the United States, signed
by Ronnie and Nancy.

"I didn't vote for him," Manny said, smiling wickedly.

Luncheon was over. Guests transferred napkins from laps to
tables. A few, including the mayor, hurried off to urgent business. Many stood and greeted old acquaintances.

"I have to go see Manny," Johnny said. Amelia rose and
shook hands with the Bernals, then pushed the wheelchair from
the table. Manny was in the center of the dining room, surrounded by well wishers.

"Johnny!" Manny's face beamed. "I've been looking for you
everywhere. Oh, Johnny, I'm so glad you came. God, how I love
you, Johnny."

Johnny's face brightened through the tears in his eyes. He
gripped the arms of the wheelchair and pushed himself to his
feet, leaning on the cane that took the place of his missing right
leg. "I couldn't sleep last night thinking about you," he said as
they hugged.

Amelia gave Manny a hug and kiss, then hurried toward the
nurse who was wheeling Mrs. Silva from the room. "Leonor!"
she called. The nurse stopped and looked back. "I wanted to say
hello," Amelia said to the nurse. The waxen flesh statue stared as
if whoever was trapped in there had vacated the premises.

Amelia gave Leonor a hug in spite of the aversion she felt.
How unlike the many times in the past when Leonor's sharp-
tongued greetings had brought her despair and anger. Even last
time, just before she became senile, Leonor's parting whine had
been, "Remember that birthday party when Tomás was six years
old? You were new in the neighborhood. When the party was
over and your mother came to take you home, I asked how you
liked the party. To my dying day I'll remember. 'It wasn't worth

the present,' you said. And I had worked my fingers to the bone. Chocolate cake. Ice cream. A piñata. Everything a child could ever want." Well, Leonor did not remember now. Perhaps she had already had her dying day, even though she still breathed.

When Amelia returned to Johnny, he was still standing, smiling at one of Manny's jibes. Then the younger crowd came by, including Manny's youngest grandson who extended a hand toward her. She noticed the stick-like black cross tattooed in the fleshy part between his thumb and forefinger—did he belong to some gang?—and she quickly looked away as she shook the hard young hand. Arturo, who had rushed up to the group, looked around searching. "That pompous ass brother of mine," he grumbled, darting off toward the exit.

"You're coming to the house?" Manny said. "We've hardly begun to talk." Johnny nodded and sat back on his wheelchair. Amelia pushed him out toward the parking lot.

"How does he do it?" Johnny asked as she drove their Cadillac. She could see the perplexity on his face. Alongside it, hand in hand, was the fear, and she knew that he was still thinking of death. He had told Manny that he hadn't slept last night. What he hadn't told him was that he hadn't slept in many nights. As if he was afraid that if he closed his eyes to rest, he would never open them again.

Arturo was at the door ushering in the luncheon guests who had been invited to the house, a small place, not too well kept up. "There you are," he said. "Dad's waiting for you, Johnny." Then, lowering his voice, "Here comes Francisco. He's the one from the old neighborhood who made good, but he's not stuck up a bit."

Amelia pushed the wheelchair through the door. Then she stopped, looking around the small living room. Behind her she overheard Arturo shout greetings to the Bernals, then sotto voce, "You met the Ruizes. Man, they're loaded."

The buffet was set up on the dining table. There was bean dip, tortilla chips, tiny little tamales, salsa, potato salad, tiny sausages, and more. A new, green plastic trash barrel filled with ice held chilling cans and bottles of beer and soft drinks.

Manny was sitting in the center of the living room, enthroned on a dining chair with arms. His thin little legs hung straight down, his feet hovering a few inches above the worn carpet. "Over here. Over here," he said eagerly. Amelia pushed the wheelchair toward him, moved one of the unused chairs aside, and wheeled Johnny into the vacant space.

"Manny," Johnny said. "I'm so glad to be here." He looked at the guests standing around talking, passing by the dining table, or going to the plastic barrel for something to drink. "Who are all these people?"

Manny looked at him the way he might have looked at his wife when she didn't recognize the familiar. "My nephew from Chicago. My cousin from Tucson. Arty's children from his first marriage, with their children, my great-grandchildren. And that one over there," he said playfully, pointing at the priest, still in suit coat while all of the other men were now in shirt sleeves, "that prig drinking Coca Cola is my son, Tommy. Worse even than Leonor in her prime." The skin of his apple-shiny face sagged as he shook his head sadly. "But you, Johnny. You been in the hospital. How are you?"

Johnny patted his empty trouser leg just below the knee. "Not so good. This one was difficult."

Manny looked down at the empty pants leg and placed a hand on Johnny's arm. "I wish," he said, "that they could have cut off my pecker instead of your leg."

Johnny managed a smile. Amelia went to the kitchen for a highball, then stopped by the table to select a few things that Johnny might try, arranging them on a paper plate. She exchanged a few words with Father Tom and the nephew from Chicago. She could see her husband and Manny leaning toward each other, talking intimately, like schoolgirls trading secrets.

When she returned with the plate of snacks, the Bernals were paying their respects to Manny. "Who are you again?" Manny was asking, turning his magnifying glass lenses up toward Francisco. "Oh, yes. Yes. I remember now. Arty's friend. But you used to be such a little fellow. Yes. The last time we had the poker party at the house you went home with all the money."

Francisco smiled and introduced María. "Well," Manny said. "You're a lucky fellow with such a lovely lady. Tell me, Francisco, how is your mother?"

"She died year before last, Mr. Silva."

He shook his head sadly. "I'm sorry. A lovely woman." Then

he turned bright eyes, magnified through his glasses, toward María. "Even an old man still appreciates a lovely woman."

"Old?" she said. "We're all old. As old as God and as young as the newborn day."

Manny's expression faded to one of confusion. "I don't exactly know what you said, but Francisco obviously married someone who is as smart as she is beautiful."

The Bernals exchanged smiles, held hands, and moved away toward Arty who was in the kitchen struggling with a bottle opener. When they left, Amelia sat and offered the snacks to Johnny who instead leaned toward Manny.

"Do you ever think of . . . death?" he whispered.

"All the time," Manny said. "I've even been kissed by it a few times. Like today with the gorilla. But it hasn't yet hugged me and hung on."

Johnny stared at Manny, his eyes crinkled in confusion. "How do you do it, Manny?" Manny flashed him a look. "Live so long I mean. God. What do you do all day? Since I quit work, especially since the last operation, I got nothing to do. What do you do all day?" He sounded like he was ready to cry.

"Well," Manny said matter of factly. "I call the taxi to take me to the home every morning so I can sit with Leonor. She flashes in and out like a shortwave radio. I want to be there when it turns out to be more than just static. Two dollars the cab driver charges me. I don't even have to tell him where to take me. He knows. And I do my own shopping in the supermarket. One of the grandchildren drives me every Thursday."

"But how do you keep yor mind alive? I feel like I'm turning into a vegetable. Especially with this." Johnny slapped the empty pants leg with disdain.

Manny stared as if trying to figure out what it was he was asking. "I used to play chess five or six hours a day with some of the others at the retirement home. Is that what you mean?"

"What's the secret, Manny? How did you make it through for so long?"

The puzzled look remained on Manny's face. His thin little shoulders gave a miniature shrug. "I don't know," he said. "I just wake up every day and put one foot in front of the other."

"There's got to be a secret."

"Well, Johnny. Tell me. You've made a lot of money in your life. What's the secret?"

Johnny blinked in surprise. He turned toward Amelia as if she had the answer. "Well," he said, "it isn't just hard work." Unspoken were the words: You've worked hard all your life; you know that. "I don't know. I guess— Maybe it's just that . . . I had the knack. And a little luck."

Manny spread his hands in a quick little gesture that accompanied his miniature shrug. "Yes!" he said. "Yes."

Then they started to reminisce about old times, and Manny was smiling. Johnny sat glumly, seeming to fade with fatigue as the minutes passed. Amelia took her empty plate to the kitchen and set the half-empty glass on the counter beside the sink. She stood unobserved for a moment, staring at her husband. Her mind, she realized, had already bid Johnny goodbye, much the way that Manny must have bid Leonor goodbye. But her heart had not yet accepted the inevitable, and tears flooded her eyes.

She turned away, staring out the window at the patio, until she was in control again. Then she sought out Arty and his wife and Tom to tell them that they must be going.

"It's time," she said simply to Johnny as she grasped the back of the wheelchair.

"We have to go, Manny." Johnny looked very tired now, and his words were slurred.

Manny stood carefully, gingerly, and shuffled the few steps to the wheelchair. He took Johnny's hands and leaned very slowly forward to kiss him. "Johnny," he said. "How I love you." He smiled and shook Johnny's two hands up and down the way children do when bouncing together.

"It's been wonderful," Amelia said, bussing Manny on the cheek. "May you live to be *two* hundred."

"If Social Security doesn't go bankrupt," Manny said.

Amelia pushed the wheelchair to the door. Before they left, she turned and saw Manny still standing, looking at them with intense, sad eyes. He knew that this was the last time he would see his friend, just as she did. That soon their lives would have to go on a little while without Johnny. The next time all three of them would be together would be in the Hereafter.

She turned quickly and pushed the wheelchair through the door.